MW00658396

Sweet Romance

For Every Season

Hope Bolinger ♥ Felicia Ferguson
Renee Leonard Kennedy ♥ Lori Z. Scott

END GAME Press

Sweet Romance for Every Season Anthology

End Game Press books may be purchased in bulk at special discounts for sales promotion, corporate gifts, ministry, fund-raising, or educational purposes. Special editions can also be created to specifications. For details, contact Special Sales Dept., End Game Press, P.O. Box 206, Nesbit, MS 38651 or info@endgamepress.com.

Visit our website at www.endgamepress.com.

Library of Congress Control Number: 2023930335
Hardback ISBN: 978-1-63797-092-8
PB ISBN: 978-1-63797-104-8
eBook ISBN: 978-1-63797-096-6

Cover Design by Abby Chiaradia
Interior Design by Typewriter Creative Co.

Printed in India
10 9 8 7 6 5 4 3 2 1

WHY SWEET ROMANCE FOR *EVERY* SEASON?

AS AUTHORS OF SWEET ROMANCE, WE NOTICED SOMETHING. Many sweet romance reads appeared to take place during Christmas.

Although we absolutely love the Christmas holidays, we felt bad for the other times of the year. They got neglected, spurned.

That got us thinking. What if other holidays and months could get their limelight?

After all, people fall in love all the time.

Not only do we have sweet stories from every time of year, but we have different types of love stories. Enemies to lovers, friends to lovers, rekindled flames, first kisses, and spark of something new.

We have a little something for everyone.

So buckle up, and enjoy sweet romance, this season, and every time of the year.

JANUARY

♥ ♥ ♥

ADORABLE

LORI Z. SCOTT

THE JONAS BROTHERS WOKE ASHLEY LIKE A BUCKET OF ice water.

At least, their ringtone song "Cool" did.

Heart pounding, Ashley slapped the nightstand until she located her cellphone and pressed it to her ear. "Hello?"

"Ashley! You're up!" Erik's voice boomed into her ear.

Roughing a hand across her face, Ashley glanced at the clock. What was her best friend thinking? "It's way too early in the morning for conversation."

"Yeah, but guess what?" He blew past her comment with his usual eagerness. "I got Linda's phone number last night."

Ashley searched her memory and drew a blank. "Who's Linda?"

"The loud brunette in the group of late-night single ladies I waited on last night."

Ah. The rowdy table near the bar. New Year's Eve always brought crowds to the restaurant. Ashley didn't remember a brunette though. Just a squad of overdressed Barbies. "And you called to tell me this at 6:32 in the morning the day after New Year's Eve because ... why?"

"I'm desperate for advice on females. What should I do?"

"Go back to sleep. I am." Ashley yawned for emphasis. "Bye."

"No, I mean, where would we go if I asked her out?" Erik's voice held a hint of panic. "Do you think she'd like tickets to *The Lion King?"*

"A musical?" Ashley scoffed. "Why would you do that? I had to drag you to see *Wicked.* And you complained the whole time."

"Well, if your boyfriend wasn't such a wimp, he would have sucked it up and gone instead. Besides, it worked out okay for me." Erik's voice held a hint of mischief. "I secretly liked it. Made me feel *popular."*

Give the boy credit for paying attention to the lyrics.

"Yes. Well." Ashley flopped back into her mattress and stared at the popcorn ceiling. "I never expected Brent to go for something like that. It's not his thing."

"And yet, you bought two tickets." Erik didn't hide his sarcasm.

A tight knot formed in Ashley's stomach.

She pulled her covers up to her chin. "It made sense to get two. Just in case he decided to go."

"The way you went to rodeos and pretended to enjoy them?" Erik clicked his tongue. "Do you even know what steer wrestling is?"

"Oh, quit!" Ashley frowned at the phone. "This is about you, not me. Now, let me think."

Erik quieted, but she could almost feel his tension.

Chewing her lip, she considered the situation. Erik might have a date. Good, right? He was a blast to hang out with, even at work. Yet in all the time she had known him, he hadn't shown an interest in dating. When she tried to set him up with her friends, he always made an excuse to back out. Why now the sudden urgency? What was it about this girl Linda who had caught his attention?

"Well." Erik cut into her musings. Patience was never one of his virtues. "Ideas?"

Ashley didn't want him to get hurt. Best he just be himself. "No theater. You should dress up like Harry Potter and take her to Comic-Con. Play video games. Or relax on the couch, eat popcorn, and binge watch reruns of *Star Trek*. If the girl sticks around after all that, she's a keeper."

"Is there an option four?"

Ashley sighed. "Goodnight, Erik." She dropped the phone on the nightstand and pulled a pillow over her head.

Two minutes later, pounding sounded on Ashley's apartment door.

"Go away, Erik!" The sheets muffled her voice. "I'm trying to sleep."

More pounding.

"Okay! I'm coming!" Gritting her teeth, Ashley threw off the covers and stepped barefoot onto the cold wooden floor. She was almost to the entry before she realized all she had on was a t-shirt and undies.

The pounding continued as she stomped back to her room, grabbed a Pokémon bathrobe, wrapped it around her body, and stomped back.

She yanked open the door like a stuck zipper. "What?"

Erik stood in the hallway with his fist frozen in the air. "Hello."

Ashley planted her hands on her hips and narrowed

her eyes. "What part of 'too early in the morning for conversation' do you not understand?"

Erik stepped past her. "All of it." He closed the door behind him. "So is there a number you call to order Broadway tickets? Or how does that work?"

Ashley blew out a raspberry and headed for the couch. "I'm not telling you, dude."

"No, no, no! C'mon." Erik followed her to the sofa and plopped down beside her like a puppy begging for a treat. "You've got to help me here."

"No, I don't." Ashley put force behind her words. "I'm not in charge of your love life. I'm barely in charge of my own."

"Brent's loss for breaking up with you." Erik patted her cheek. "You're adorable."

Face heating, she pushed his arm away. "Thanks, I guess."

Erik was adorable too, in his own way. Awkward in his movements, as if puberty hadn't yet released full control of twenty-five-year-old limbs yet. Six-foot-two with the lean build of a gamer. A generous but crooked smile. A decent blond beard. Untrimmed hair he flicked to keep out of his blue eyes, which were surrounded by lashes so pale that it looked like someone had dusted them with flour. He could have passed as a Viking character in the movie *How to Train Your Dragon*.

Still. Her? Adorable? "I wish you had told that to Brent."

"I did. Two weeks ago, when he picked you up in a parking lot." He shrugged. "I said, 'Hey, Gorilla, don't break Ashley's heart. She's freaking adorable.'"

"And?" She leaned in. "What did he say?"

"He ignored me."

"Big surprise." Ashley curled her legs under her. "Did

you ever consider that it might be your sardonic delivery that gave him doubts?"

"No. I think it's the fact that I used big words when I leaked the additional information that you bought a new pair of cowboy boots with decorative tooling and a cattleman hat with a braided hat band and stayed up until three o'clock the day before the rodeo to find out if barrel racing was anything like what Hobbits do in a river when trying to escape wood elves and orcs. Which was—" He paused his deluge of words to gasp air and lifted a finger. "—adorable."

Ashley snorted. "For your information, dork, I liked Brent. I still do."

"Yes, but is Brent adorable?" Erik raised his brows.

She pushed him away again. "Just don't take Linda to the theater unless you were serious about liking it."

"Okay, fine." Erik crossed his arms. "No theater. But you're a girl. What do girls like?"

"I don't know! Depends on the girl." Ashley closed her eyes and drew a deep breath. "You should ask yourself, 'What does Linda like?'"

"Well ..." Erik rubbed his beard. "I only talked to her for the span of a meal with seven other chatty girls while I was waiting on three more tables. All I know is she likes her steak medium-rare, and—" He pointed at himself. "—her waiters extra spicy."

"Hold on a minute." Ashley sat up straight. "Are you actually going to ask this girl out?"

"Maybe." Erik tugged the edge of his shirt. "Soon."

Ashley growled. "You mean never." She stood and pulled on Erik's arm. Then she dragged him to his feet, put both hands on his back, and steered him across the room. "Good night, Erik. Here's the front door." She opened it and pushed him out. "I'm going back to sleep. I'll see you at work tomorrow."

He blocked the door with his foot. "Wrong. You'll see me tonight at five when the Rose Bowl starts. We planned this, remember? I'm pulling for Oregon, you're rooting for Michigan, and I'm bringing the pizza."

"With—"

"I know. Thin crust, pepperoni and olives, extra cheese, and a Diet Coke." Erik flashed two thumbs-up. "I got you covered."

Ashley closed the door, leaned against it, and smiled. Erik drove her crazy with his high energy and fast talking. But he really was adorable sometimes. Especially when he brought her pizza.

♥ ♥ ♥

In Ashley's opinion, January 2 was only slightly better than eating raw onions. It marked the beginning of a dry spell of holidays between December winter festivities and February's Valentines's Day. True, there was Martin Luther King Jr. Day on the sixteenth, but until that holiday involved fireworks, presents, piñatas, Hallmark cards, eggnog, or chocolate, Ashley wouldn't be requesting vacation time.

In other words, work was all she had to look forward to for the next month. At least working with Erik would make it bearable.

After tying her tan half-apron over her generic black waitstaff uniform, Ashley loaded the front pouch with a small notepad, a pen, and her phone. Then she twisted her black hair into a high ponytail. The four-star restaurant promised to be busy tonight.

Erik had been signed up for the same three-to-nine p.m. shift, and she waved at him when he joined the floor. Despite his flaws, she appreciated his friendship. He knew how upset she was after Brent texted that "things weren't working out between them" and he had gone out of his way to boost her confidence. No doubt the bowl game was his attempt to keep her mind off the breakup.

But, truth be told, she had enjoyed watching the Rose Bowl with him. They had slummed around in comfortable sweatpants and collegiate shirts all night. Michigan won, an added bonus. Erik even came over early to catch the Rose Bowl parade. When they got bored of the marching bands, they played a game of Five Crowns to occupy themselves before kickoff.

At one point, Erik had laid out a run of five cards, discarded, and smirked at her. "Hardest round, and I aced it. Do you think Brent could beat that?"

Ashley shook away the memory. Brent didn't play cards. *But he sure was a good kisser! And athletic. And ...*

Maybe if she had played her cards right with him, she would still have a boyfriend.

Erik nudged her. "You gonna daydream all night? Ironic."

Even though he wore the same half apron and uniform as she did, he still somehow managed to look decent. *Must be the cut.*

"Come on, Spacey," he said. "Those tips aren't going to earn themselves. We've got customers."

And so, the daily grind began. It started slowly with the happy hour crowd, then picked up as the evening progressed. Patrons ordered drinks and salads and appetizers and entrees, and the wait crew floated between them like synchronized hummingbirds.

Ashley was running a credit card payment when Brent walked in with some floozy hanging on his arm. The girl wore a short denim dress, bright red lipstick, and cowboy boots.

Ice filled Ashley's veins, and she ducked behind the

register. "Natalie," she said to the hostess. "Mind if I ring this one up myself?"

"Be my guest." Natalie stepped back, attention already on the next client.

Peeking out, Ashley saw Brent whisper something in the girl's ear. The chica put her free hand to her mouth, laughed, then stood on tiptoe to whisper something back. Classic flirt body language.

Gee, it didn't take long for him to move on. Ashley narrowed her eyes and tracked Brent's progress across the room. He'd be seated soon. *Please, not in my section.* She'd never told him where she worked. To have to wait on him now ... No, it would be too humiliating. She needed a plan of action. No way she'd leave Brent in the clutches of a cowgirl without a fight.

Ashley searched the room. The smell of basil and garlic flavored the air while low instrumental music enhanced the intimate setting. Couples leaned together, sharing the passion of a savory meal.

How would Brent react if he saw her all cozied up with another man tonight in the same restaurant? Could she make him jealous enough to want her back?

Not dressed like a waitress.

Sudden memory made her pulse race. Last week, Erik had been raving about how much better the *Game of Thrones* books were than the television series, and Ashley planned to walk to the library after work and check out the first book. Except she ended up reserving an audio version instead, negating the need to visit the library. That left the short skirt and blouse she brought to change into still jammed in her locker.

This could work. All she needed was a date.

Using a menu to hide her face, she made a beeline for Erik and grabbed his arm.

"Hey!" Erik jumped, nearly spilling his load. "Watch it. I'm delivering a chicken fettuccine here."

She bowed her head, trying to stay out of Brent's line of sight. "Do you have clean clothes in your locker?"

Erik frowned. "Maybe a sweater."

"It will do." She gave a furtive glance at the waiting line. "Come with me to the staging area."

"I'm kinda busy." He nodded at the platter in his hands. The steam from it made sweat bead on his lip. "Can it wait?"

Ashley ground her teeth together. She still had customers too, but she couldn't go on the floor and finish serving her tables. The risk of Brent spotting her was too great.

"I can wait." She released her grip. "But I have a huge favor to ask. Can you finish my shift?"

Erik pulled a hand towel from his apron and blotted his forehead. "Let me get this straight. You want me to cover my four tables ... and your four tables? What do I get out of it?"

"I'll bake you cookies." Food always made a good bribe.

Brows lowered, Erik scanned the dinner crowd. "You've got two squirmy kids and a grandma with an attitude. I deserve a back massage too."

"You drive a hard bargain." Ashley surrendered her tabs and hustled toward the changing area.

Twenty minutes later, she was applying mascara when Erik stumbled through the door. Sweat glistened on his face and dampened his neck. He whistled as he lowered himself onto the lone bench in the small space and held out a handful of one-dollar bills. "I brought your tips. Most were credit card, but this is what the table with the two kids left you. Well, this and a stick of gum. I kept the gum." He popped the chewy substance between his teeth.

"You could have kept it all."

"And risk my cookie deal?" Erik shook his head. "Nope."

He eyeballed her. "Wow, you look and you smell like vanilla. Whatever trouble you're into, it better be worth it."

With her finger, Ashley dabbed on a shimmer of lipstick. "If I can get Brent back, it will be totally worth you pretending to be my boyfriend."

"Brent again?" Erik's face paled. "And I'm your what?"

"My boyfriend." Gripping the front of his shirt, Ashley yanked him closer. "Look, Brent is out there, right now, on a date." She pointed to the doorway. "And I'm going out there looking hot with my sophisticated boyfriend." She inclined her head to Erik. "He'll get jealous and want me back."

"Sinister. Doomed. And also potentially hilarious." Erik nodded. "I like your style."

Ashley slapped his chest. "Just look cute and buy me dinner."

"Wait. Buying dinner wasn't part of the deal. Have you seen the menu prices? Ouch!"

"My treat then. But first, I need to practice something. Hold still." Ashley raised a brow and let her lips curve into a seductive smile. But since it was Erik staring back at her, she couldn't hold the pose. What if she ran a finger down his arm?

"Oh! You're giving me goosebumps!" Erik shivered. "Stop it!"

Suddenly uncomfortable, Ashley pulled her hand back. Some temptress she turned out to be. "I'll work on it. Meanwhile, you clean up. We find where Brent's located. We convince Natalie to seat us at an open table nearby. And then we order. And you can tell me a joke. And I'll laugh and—"

"Dang, girl, I'll never remember all that. How about we just wing it?"

Like improv. Any theater lover could pull that off, right? "Sure. Now, let's work on you." Ashley sized him up. "The black pants will do. Where is that sweater you were talking about?"

"You mean the one with Yoda dressed up like Santa Claus?" Erik quirked an eyebrow.

"Never mind. I'll get creative with the extra uniforms." She mushed his hair to one side, then the other. "Then we'll style that mop."

Light music played when the two strolled out arm in arm. Nervous as Ashley was about her plan, Erik's warmth lent her comfort.

As Natalie seated them, Ashley zeroed in on Brent. He hadn't noticed her. Not yet, anyway.

"Catch!" Erik blew her a kiss, then whispered, "How am I doing?"

"You're perfect." She giggled and laid her hand on his wrist. "Be still my heart."

Was Brent watching? Stoking her curiosity, she stroked Erik's beard. "You're sweet. And funny. A real knight in shining armor."

"And you're smart. And beautiful. So beautiful. Like a beige lampshade."

A beige lampshade?

The tease in his eyes made it hard to keep a straight face. "Tell me more." She fluttered her eyelashes at him. "And?"

"And I think you've got something in your eyes."

"It's called a facial tick, darling." She brought his hand to her lips and kissed his fingers one by one. "It's caused by excess joking."

Erik smiled and leaned forward. Ashley followed suit until they were nose to nose.

"What are you doing?" Erik kept his gaze on the couple beyond them.

"I'm flirting," she said, giving his fingertip a playful nip. "Is Brent watching?"

"Nope." Erik's breath was warm on her neck. "Maybe you should do my other hand."

"Okay." She traced his arm, following the contours to his other hand. "Hmm, you've got a few muscles under there." *Kiss*. *Kiss*. "Have you been working out?"

"Lamest line ever, don't use that on Brent," Erik said. "But, yes, I did stack several heavy boxes of Kleenex in my storage unit last Saturday. And I hefted my game controller like a million times."

"Mmmm. That sounds even lamer." Between kisses, Ashley chanced a sultry look over her shoulder. Yes, Brent was watching.

"That feels soooooo nice." Erik purred. "I just have one question for you."

"Anything," Ashley whispered.

"Don't you want to know if I washed those hands before you put them in your mouth?"

She gasped. "What?!"

"Gotcha." Erik smirked.

Oh, that troublemaker. He was having fun with this. Narrowing her eyes, she flicked his cheek with her finger. "You dork."

"Let me show you how sexy is done." Erik flipped his hair, pinched his lips and stared at her. Slowly, he raised one brow.

She stifled a laugh. "You look constipated."

"Wrong. That's my smoldering gaze."

"Well, don't use that fire in the bathroom." She bit her lip. "You might cause a gas explosion."

"Ha!" Erik's quick laugh tickled her senses, and she joined him.

"Quit dissing my moves," he said when she caught her breath. "How am I supposed to act?"

Poor guy. He didn't have much experience. Maybe she shouldn't have put him in such an awkward position.

Reaching out, she brushed back a strand of his unruly hair, then lowered her hand to cup his chin. He really was adorable.

"Okay." Erik's cheeks reddened, and he pulled away. "That fake flirting you just did there? Much better. Very believable. I feel loved."

Was she faking it that time?

Where had that thought come from? She quickly dropped her hands into her lap.

Brent. Focus on Brent.

"Hello, I'm Marco, and I'll be your server tonight. Can I start you off with some drinks?" Marco nodded at Ashley and winked at Erik. Natalie must have sent him.

"Yes, drinks would be nice." Ashley hoped her voice would carry over the sound of nearby conversations. "I want Diet Coke and he'll have a sweet tea."

Erik unfolded his napkin. "And an order of fried mushrooms with ranch dip and two orders of spaghetti with meatballs. Lots of parmesan on top. You're cool with that, right Ash?"

"You know me too well." She nodded her agreement.

Marco jotted down their order and hustled away.

A shadow darkened the tablecloth, and Ashley tensed. She shot Erik a desperate, wide-eyed look. *Brent?* she mouthed.

His face fell. He hesitated, then gave a slight nod.

Ashley broke eye contact with Erik and lifted her chin. "Brent? What are you doing here?"

"Ashley." Brent bent and kissed her cheek. "I thought I recognized that voice. Do you come here a lot? It sounds like you've got the menu memorized."

"*We* come here all the time." Erik stood with just the right amount of protective boyfriend gruffness and extended his hand. "I'm Erik. Ashley's *boyfriend*."

"You look familiar." Brent said, furrowing his brow. "I

know! Owen Wilson without the crooked nose." He waved Erik off and grabbed a chair from his table. "Mind if we join you?"

"Since you already have, I guess not." Erik gestured at the denim-dressed girl, offering his seat. "Next to photo-bombing, meal crashing's the big thing. Congrats on joining the trend."

Totally missing Erik's sarcasm, the girl flashed a toothy smile and sat down. "Thanks. You're cute. I'm Fiona, by the way. Brent's *girlfriend."*

"I like how you stretched it out there." Brent swept his hand in an arch. "Girlfriend." He nabbed another chair and lowered himself into it. "It flows like a waterslide. Girlfriend." He motioned again. "See? Nice and smooth."

Fiona tittered and touched the tip of Erik's nose with a red-lacquered fingernail. "Aren't you adorable?"

Bristling, Ashley clenched her fists. *That's my best friend, lady. Be nice.*

"Yes. Yes, I am adorable." Erik shot Ashley a look that said *you owe me big time* and drew a sharp breath. "I'm like a puppy and a baby seal all rolled into one." Erik planted both elbows on the table and wedged his chin between his hands. "So. Fiona. Tell me about yourself, *girlfriend."*

Fiona was either a little tipsy or Erik was in rare form, because she warmed up to him fast. Or, was it Ashley's imagination, but was Erik being—*charming?*

Not wanting to stray from her plan, Ashley tore her attention away from Erik's gut-busting facial expressions and turned to Brent. She'd planned a thousand ways to start this conversation, but settled on, "Hello."

"You look good," Brent said without missing a beat.

"Thanks." Ashley drank in his square jaw and chiseled physique. Even his voice seemed capable of bench pressing a horse. "So do you."

Leering, Brent put a hand on her knee. Every nerve ending in her skin flared to life at his touch. And yet it felt oddly dirty too. The heady scent of his cologne bridged the distance between them. "You know, if you'd dressed like that all the time, I never would've lost your phone number."

Should I be flattered or slap him for that comment? "Your text made it clear you didn't need my phone number anymore." Ashley attempted a coy smile. "Or do you?"

"Oh, I need something all right." He jerked his head sideways. "But it looks like you've already moved on with Wonder Boy."

"You mean Erik?" Ashley glanced at her friend.

Fiona was ruffling his hair. "I love how soft it feels. Can I braid it?"

Help me, Erik mouthed.

Chest tightening, Ashley frowned. Couldn't the girl keep her hands to herself?

Brent snapped his fingers to recapture her attention. "Yes, I mean Erik."

Ashley considered her words. "We've become very close. What about you and this Fiona girl? It seems you moved on too."

"This ain't my first rodeo." Brent licked his lips. "Let's just say I always get back on the horse. But when they start turning into old nags, it's time to saddle up another. Like you."

Indecision seized her. Sure, she wanted Brent back. He was confident and attractive. A man's man. But how could he talk that way right in front of his date? Erik would never do that to a girl.

Erik's unsuccessful attempts to fend off Fiona distracted Ashley. Red lipstick smudged one of his cheeks. But, though clearly uncomfortable with Fiona's attention, he endured it. Why?

Because I asked him to.

Her gut twisted. Sure, there were cookies and a massage involved too, but she felt certain he would have done it for her anyway. Because he cared about how she felt, even at his own expense.

Brent gripped her arm, still talking to her apparently. "So, I say we ditch the witch." He laughed at his own rhyme. "And then you can hitch a ride home with me instead. Sound good?"

Marco appeared before she could reply. "Your drinks!" He slammed the Diet Coke and sweet tea down with such force, they tipped over. Brent jumped to his feet, but too late. Ice and soda drenched the front of his pants. He let loose a stream of profanities worthy of a cowhand.

Heart pounding, Ashley took in the scene. Was this the man she really wanted? She swallowed hard. "I think you should go now."

"Don't have much of a choice, do I?" Brent brushed at his wet pants. "I'll call you later."

Erik's face fell.

So did Ashley's stomach. "No."

"What?" Brent paused mid-step.

Ashley squared her shoulders. "Brent, do you know my favorite college football team? What book I just read?" She locked eyes with Erik. "My favorite appetizer?"

"Who cares about that crap?"

"I do." Ashley pointed at Erik. "And he does."

"Him?" Brent scowled and flexed his bicep. "You're joking. You'd pick him over me?"

Anger bubbled up in her at the implied insult. She clenched her teeth. "Yes. No joke."

Erik looked to the right and the left and then pointed at himself. "Me?"

Ashley nodded. "You're adorable."

Face reddening, Brent worked his jaw. "Fine. Come on, Fiona. Let's get out of this dump."

"Get along, little doggie." Erik gave a dainty wave with his fingers. When Brent reached the door, he yelled, "And for your information, Ashley hates rodeos."

As soon as the door closed behind them, Ashley and Erik burst out laughing.

"Did you see the look on his face?" Ashley asked.

"No." Erik let out a strangled *pff-pff-pff* kind of laugh. "I was too busy looking at his pants! Marco, you nailed it!" He gave the waiter a high-five. "I owe you one."

"Marco!" Ashley's eyes widened. "What did you do?"

The man grinned. "If things went south, Erik gave me specific directions on how to intervene."

Ashley smoothed down her shirt, letting her thoughts pick their way through the Mines of Moria. She remembered the rush of excitement she felt on her first date with Brent. Now she remembered his callousness. What she had hoped for in the relationship and the reality were quite different. She'd fooled herself. "Were you rescuing Erik or me from the Balrog?" she asked.

Erik shook his head. "Marco won't understand your *Lord of the Rings* reference," he whispered. "Let's just say he rescued both of us from your horrid choice in men and move on."

"My shift is almost over," Marco said. "Are you two going to continue with this fake date?"

Ashley fidgeted with the soda-splattered spoon, twisting it in circles. "No." She lifted her gaze, matching Erik's stare. "Unless you want to make it—"

"—a real date?" Erik's words stole her breath. Was he joking or serious?

Mind racing, Ashley closed her eyes. She tried to picture herself with Brent, but only saw Erik. It has always been Erik, hadn't it? Erik, who, when he'd seen her interest in theater, bought the soundtrack to *Wicked* and learned the lyrics from every song so they could lip-sync together in the living room. Erik, who played cards with her on rainy days. Erik, who brought her soup when she felt sick.

Erik, who knew as much about *The Hobbit* as she did.

A guy who stuck around after all that was a keeper.

She opened her eyes. "Yes, a real date. I'd like that."

"Me too." Erik's voice was oddly hoarse.

"Marco, you'd better bring us more drinks to go with our dinner." Ashley righted the empty cups. "After all, someone's spaghetti and meatballs are on the line."

"On it!" Marco took his cue and left.

Ashley snagged a napkin and stepped closer to Erik. "Thanks for always looking out for me."

His Adam's apple bobbed, and he shifted his gaze away. "That's what friends are for, right?"

Friends. Somehow the word carried a different meaning to her now.

"Hold still. You've got Fiona's lipstick on your cheek." She dabbed at his face. His body seemed to tremble at her touch. "And I want my lipstick to be there instead."

She planted a lingering kiss on his cheek. "Boyfriend."

A slow smile spread across his face. "I like the sound of that. Boyfriend. It flows like a waterslide."

She elbowed him. "Dork."

"That's 'adorable dork' to you." He laid a hand over his heart. "And don't forget. Someone still owes me cookies and a massage."

Lowering herself into the chair, she clicked her tongue. "You can collect when you come over for the Orange Bowl."

"Sweats and pizza?" he asked.

"Yep, sweats and pizza."

"Double or nothing on the massage if Texas A&M wins?" He cocked his head.

She raised a brow. "Double regardless of who wins."

FEBRUARY

♥ ♥ ♥

MARTYR'S DAY

ROSE HATHAWAY

THEY SAY THERE ARE TWO TYPES OF WOMEN ON Valentine's Day.

Type One: The kind who wear red puffy sweaters bedazzled in sequin hearts. Those who jump onto social media to immediately upload photos of the heart-shaped boxes their beau sent them. The ones who would consider it a crime if their man had the audacity to forget a holiday greeting card invention of a holiday.

Type Two: Enter me.

I slather another layer of dark eyeliner on my waterline.

Do I look goth enough? Goodness, even at twenty-seven, I could pass for an emo teen ... if not for the bags under my eyes and fine lines beginning to form near my mouth.

I step back and take a gander at my "mourning dress." A lacy monstrosity I picked up at a thrift store that I imagine a person playing a widow in a stage play would wear.

The dramatic webbing of fabric cascades all the way to the floor.

We'll draw some eyes with this number.

"Good." My lips curl. I painted them black today. "Anything for St. V."

See, most single gals like me celebrate an alternative holiday to Valentine's Day. Some may gather their favorite girl friends and partake in a brunch labeled "Galentine's Day." Others may abashedly share a meme on social media, with their hearts going out to all of those having to suffer "Singleness Awareness Day."

Me?

I partake in a new holiday. One I spotted in a social media post during my college days.

Celibate Catholic Martyr's Day. CCMD, for short.

Celibate because, well, St. Valentine never got married. At least, according to most accounts.

Catholic, because, take your wildest guess about St. V's denomination.

Martyr. Beaten by clubs, nasty way to go.

Day, you get the point.

I snap a mirror selfie and shoot a message to my best friend. She's decided to partake in Singleness Awareness Day by planting herself in front of her latest Netflix binge with a tub of ice cream cradled in her palms.

Her response glitters on the screen. "Represent, Claudia. Make us singles proud."

I feel my dimples bore into my cheeks, I'm smiling so wide. "Oh, don't worry. I will." And I'll document the whole thing on social media too—despite my mother's begging for me to stop posting about singleness.

"It'll drive away any prospects you have left."

Don't worry, mother dearest, after plenty of dating app escapes, blind date setups, and you name it, I don't even believe there are any so-called "suitors" left. Just like

Valentine's Day, the love men claim to have is "fake." A sham to sell more chocolates and flowers.

Snowflakes flurry outside my apartment as I scrape off my car and then head to my first destination: a local brunch spot, Best of the Brunch.

From what I've learned in past Februarys, couples swarm the place during the morning. I crash in through the doors and notice most tables are occupied with men and women decked in pink and red. Poor waiters heap their arms in plate loads of avocado toast and pink pancakes in the shape of hearts.

Eyes train on me.

I hold my head up high and ask the hostesses for a table for one. She grimaces, and I think I catch a flicker of a spark in her eyes. Maybe she appreciates my outfit choice. She certainly glances me up and down several times, probably thinking I don't notice.

"This way."

She wedges me into a corner booth toward the back of the restaurant. Smart choice, away from the view of most paying customers. I spy only one other lone customer who doesn't bedeck himself in burning bright colors.

A corner booth across from me hosts a man in a dark coat and sunglasses. Why the shades? I glimpse the window beside me, decorated in strings of hearts. Slate skies blanket the area surrounding the eatery.

Even though the shades cover his retinas, I catch him stealing glances my way.

I flip open the menu. My eyes land on some beauty of French toast with banana-walnut topping. Then I close the booklet and slap the laminated thing on the table.

He hasn't stopped staring. I take out my phone and pull open the LIVE button for the social media app of my choice.

"Hey, everyone. Claudia here. Updating you on

my Celibate Catholic Martyr's Day adventures. Since Valentine's Day is a sham, and the best way to remember St. V. is not by giving each other chocolates, but by mourning his brutal death."

I flip the screen to face the packed crowd and display the plethora of pink couples.

"Our first destination is this brunch place. I've drawn the attention of quite a few patrons. All for the cause."

After I end the LIVE stream, my skin bubbles when I feel the burn of the guy's gaze continuing to flit in my direction.

"Can I help you, dude?"

He slackens on his seat, grimaces. "Sorry. Name's Rhys. I couldn't help but overhear you. Did you say that Valentine's Day is purely for commercialization?"

My spine straightens against the cushy booth seat. Relax, Claudia. The whole point of you going out in this heavy metal getup is to start conversations. Make people recognize the invisible singles on this day.

One by one, my fingertips prattle on my menu. "Yep. Valentine wasn't ever married. He did help *marry* people. But everyone has turned his holiday of remembrance into an excuse to humble-brag about their spouse or significant other on social media."

I can't stop my eyes flicking to the empty spot across from him. Had I insulted his date? Did his date already make a post this morning about him?

His neck snaps to the vacant spot and back to me.

"Pretty sure she ditched. It's been half an hour, and she won't respond to my texts." He grips his neck. "This was my fault for allowing my friends to set me up on a blind date for Valentine's—celibate whatever-you-call-it day."

You know, without that grimace and those sunglasses, that hair and that deep olive skin tone could really pass for cute. The deep voice certainly does.

"Sorr—" My apology gets cut off by the server who stops by my table to take my order. When she fades from view, I finish the "sorry." And then, "I know we just met, but if you'd like some new plans to make up for a date ditching you ..."

I explain my itinerary for the day. He brightens. Even despite the shades, I swear I can spot some optical beauties underneath those.

"Yeah, you know what, Claudia, that does sound fun. Where do you go after this destination?"

Our next pit stop finds us on a hiking trail. Many couples propose on the overlook, a rocky ledge that sits atop an ocean of trees. In the autumn, the foliage bursts into a firework of red and orange leaves.

On the way, we discuss occupations, dreams, the usual questions to make sure the other person isn't a serial killer. Slushy snow drags on my dress, but I don't mind.

When we reach the overlook, a literal line of couples snakes into the trees for a center spot on the rock. We catch the lucky ones—the man and woman who finally made it to overlook—mid-proposal.

Rhys snickers into his knuckles. He whispers to me, "This is hilarious. Proposals are supposed to be a surprise. But they—" he motions to the queue, "—are literally *waiting* to be 'surprised.'"

Dragon's breath trails from my nostrils as I try to hold in giggles.

We find a spot at the back of the line and make a slow trek to the front. When we finally reach the rock, I LIVE-shoot the "proposal" Rhys has prepared for me. He gets down on one knee and hands me a stick from the frozen ground next to him.

"Will you, Claudia, be my Celibate Catholic Martyr's Day girlfriend for today as we unveil the counterfeit nature of this holiday?"

I clasp my hands to my mouth and pretend like he's knocked the wind out of me as I double over. "Yes, yes! A thousand times yes."

He slides the stick into my black-gloved hand, and a smattering of confused applause sounds off from behind us. When we escape the rock, another couple supplants us.

Destination three: A popular sandwich joint, where they offer a special of heart-shaped cheese curds. Set in a college town, we gather quite the crowd around our table as Rhys delivers a heartfelt lecture on the dangers of commercialism.

Destination four: A movie theater, where we catch the latest rom-com flick and pellet each other with popcorn when the other person isn't looking.

Destination five: A coffee shop, where frugal Valentine's Day couples split the cost of a cup of pink peppermint hot cocoa. We order, "Coffee. As black as our souls. And the garments that Claudia wears, for mourning." After we decide that we hate black coffee, we order the pink monstrosity. Not bad, too much whipped cream.

(Of course, we documented all these "dates" for social media. Comments litter my screen about 'this mysterious man in a coat.' Rhys says that half my friends and family already friend-requested him. Laying it on a little thick, guys).

However, if he happened to ask me out ...

My cheeks burn at the thought. But then again, no one has ever made me laugh as much or had as deep of conversations with me in a long, long time.

Our final destination lands us in an expensive restaurant with a three-hour wait. The host up front mutters under his breath about couples who didn't call in for reservations months in advance.

Rhys and I pass the time in the plush carpeted lobby

by playing with a waterproof card deck he fished out of his pocket.

By the time we hit the three hours, others waiting have joined us in a rousing game of Egyptian Ratscrew.

A server escorts us to our table, where my eyes bulge at the prices on the menu. Good thing he and I have paid for ourselves separately today. Guilt would gnaw at my gut if a man had to pay thirty-five dollars for a steak for me.

"So." Rhys fiddles with the buttons on his jacket. He hasn't unsheathed that or the shades the whole day. "I have a confession to make."

My eyebrows scrunch. I clack the menu against the table. "Go on."

He tugs at the collar of his coat and flicks his gaze toward the heart-shaped strings of lights that hang from the wooden ceiling beams like vines. A fireplace nearby our high top crackles.

"When I said I had a date ditch me earlier. That wasn't true. I—" He unbuttons his jacket and unveils a dark t-shirt and black jeans underneath. "I was celebrating Celibate Catholic Martyr's Day too. I'd seen a number of social media posts about it and thought I'd give it a try, but—"

He tears off the sunglasses. Brilliant green eyes, slathered in smeared eyeliner, pierce me.

"—but when I got to the brunch place, I was embarrassed. Everyone looked like they wanted to murder me for ruining their day with dark clothing. The waitress stuck me in a booth where she could hide me ... so I covered up."

I lace my fingers together and press my chin against them. In a similar look to the way Beth Harmon did in *The Queen's Gambit*. "Go on."

"Then you walked in. And I saw you were celebrating too, and ..." His olive cheeks darken. "I was afraid to ask if you wanted someone to go with you on all of your outings. But then you offered and—I figured by then it was too late to reveal—" he motions to his makeup, "—all of this."

A heavy silence fills the air. A server rushes past with a tray full of chocolate lava cakes.

"So." I draw out the word. "You were celebrating Martyr's Day too." Something inside of me lights up. "Honestly, I'm glad I had someone to do it with. The stares can be hard to endure by yourself, aren't they?"

Heat bubbles under my skin as I blink away the memories of the brunch place.

For the rest of today, with Rhys, I truly hadn't noticed the gawks, the eye rolls, the head cocks. Those still happened, thanks to the goth makeup. But he made them more bearable.

"Yeah." He laughs. "Although, it could just be me, but I wouldn't mind doing this again. On a day that isn't Valentine's Day."

He winces, perhaps anticipating a swift rejection, and turtles himself into his t-shirt.

"You know, Rhys, I'd be fine with that. But." I raise a finger. "We must promise to never wear pink."

He places his hand on his heart, like a pledge. "I wouldn't dare."

MARCH

WHEN IRISH EYES ARE SMILING

LORI Z. SCOTT

ALEXANDRA SWEPT THE JAGGED PIECES OF HER GRANDmother's ceramic urn into the dustpan. "It would've been nice to sprinkle your ashes in the ocean like you requested," she said, dumping the particles in the trash can. "But you'll have to settle for the local landfill now."

It wasn't unusual for Alex to shatter something precious during her weekly cleaning routine, but poor Granny was a new low.

After saying a quick prayer for the sake of her dearly-now-twice departed, Alex pulled out the note app on her cell phone. The cracked screen had seen better days, but it still worked. Frowning, Alex scrolled to the document titled "failures" she had started after her last breakup.

"Don't beat yourself up over Mike," her friend Hope had said. "He's not worth it."

Maybe not. But she had downloaded the app, dug into her memories, and made the file anyway.

It really was an impressive list, starting with "swallowing the only key to mom's car" at eighteen months and ending with "dropping a houseplant on the boss's computer" just yesterday. She'd forgotten to add "lost job," but, on the bright side, now she had plenty of time to remedy that oversight.

Puckering her lips, she clicked the microphone icon. "Knocked Granny off the table with a wooden spoon while lip-syncing 'Holding Out for a Hero' instead of doing a job search."

Task completed, Alex sighed and tossed her phone on the couch. The device bounced and knocked over a half-empty coffee mug. Gasping, she righted the cup. Seconds later, the ornery phone vibrated, and the "Imperial March" ringtone sounded. *Dumb-dumb-dumb, da-da dumb, da-da dumb.*

It was Hope. "Girl, heard about the job. Sorry."

Alex's throat tightened, and she gulped to loosen it. "It's okay." She cradled the phone with her neck and dabbed the spreading brew splotch with a napkin. "I needed a fresh start anyway. Besides, I'm pretty sure I misfiled the paperwork for the last vehicle registration, so yeah. News flash. Job loss imminent."

"Why don't you apply for a graphic design position?" Hope's voice rose an octave, as if the idea excited her. "That way you can actually use your degree creating websites or selling those little picture thingies."

"You mean clipart?" Alex finished patting down the soggy cushion and covered the remaining stain with a toss pillow. "Look, I love your enthusiasm, but you know I can't pay the rent with stuff like that. To quote my mom, I need a *real* job."

"You're twenty-five, and you haven't held down a steady job or boyfriend for more than six months. If you're going to fail anyway, why not fail doing something you love?" Hope argued.

"Because without a paycheck, I can't buy food." Alex snorted. "And, for the record, if you're trying to cheer me up, you're doing a horrible job."

Hope coughed. "I really called to invite you to the Dubliner Pub on Greenville Avenue. Tonight. Downtown Dallas. Wear something green for St. Patrick's Day—unless you want to get pinched by one of my cute co-workers. Trust me, you'll be tempted. You'll come, right?"

"No. With my luck, I'll get car sick en route and actually turn green. Although, come to think of it, nothing says Irish like projectile vomit." Alex tried to make her voice sound light and airy. Like she didn't care.

"Oh, c'mon!" Hope whined. "It's an opportunity to meet new people."

No. It's an opportunity to misplace my wallet. Or swallow another car key. I'm about due for that again. "Thanks, but I'll pass." Alex pulled her shoes off. Her big toe peeked through her sock like a shy gremlin, and she wiggled it. Beyond its rounded tip, she spied a piece of Gran's crockery she'd missed. "Face it, ever since my Friday the Thirteenth birth, I'm a jinx for everyone, especially myself. The best move is to stay at home."

The phone went silent while Alex squatted to nab the missing shard—lying right next to an earring she'd lost last week.

"I'm sending a limo to pick you up at six," Hope said.

The firm clip in Hope's tone meant she wouldn't budge. Stubborn girl. Clenching her jaw, Alex glanced at the clock. 5:37. Not much time.

"Fine. I'll come. But no limo. I'll drive. And I'll wear green. But I'll pack a red shirt just in case those guys are as hot as you claim." She scooped up the last remnant of the urn and turned it over. Blood. She'd nicked her finger. "Now, leave me alone, Hope. Granny and I have some catching up to do before I get dressed."

Alex threw her phone onto the couch again, and then made a mad dash to the bathroom to put on makeup and a Band-Aid. She pulled on slim blue jeans, her favorite cowboy boots, and a green camo tank top that she covered with an unbuttoned white shirt tied at the bottom. She raked a brush through her brown waves of hair that tended to curl in an unruly way, as if they held their own reserve of static electricity. After giving herself a quick look over, she nodded. It was past six o'clock now, so ready or not, it would have to do.

Half-running, half-stumbling, she rushed down two flights of stairs. Her car roared to life, and she jerked out of the parking lot toward Interstate 30, her fastest route to downtown Big D.

Maybe an adrenaline spike caused by her frantic exit boosted her optimism, but Alex couldn't help smiling. *Maybe this will be a good night.* She clicked on the radio and let "Footloose," a classic eighties song, keep pace with her heart.

Traffic grew heavy the closer she got to the city. Alex got wedged between a monster truck shrink-wrapped to actually look like a monster—scales and all—and a semi decked with spikes and skulls reminiscent of *Mad Max's* cinematic world.

When the congestion caused her speed to drop to twenty miles per hour, then ten, then five, Alex's smile ebbed, replaced by a churning stomach. Any minute now, Hope would call her, wondering where she was, badgering her about her tardiness. She reached for her purse. At this crawl, she could safely send a quick text, right?

Digging around in the faux leather handbag produced her wallet, a taser, lipstick, gum, sanitizer in a Baby Yoda dispenser, a tissue that may or may not have been used, dental floss, a USB drive, three pens—one without a cap—an expired Sonic coupon, and a granola bar. No phone.

"No, no, no!" Gritting her teeth, Alex kept one eye on the road and rifled through the contents again. When had she last used her phone? When Hope called. After hanging up, Alex had rushed off to get ready—tossing it on the couch. Where it now lay, probably buried somewhere between the new coffee stain and her pride.

Alex gripped the wheel and rolled her head back to hit the headrest. Having no phone was like losing an arm and then getting a ghostly itch on the missing limb. An agonizing and insatiable distraction.

The least she could do was get past the cars boxing her in. Alex checked her mirror for an opening and gunned it when she saw a green Mustang lagging behind. She waved an apology to the driver she'd cut off, zoomed forward to tailgate the next car, and searched for another break in the line of traffic. Her weaving finally led to the source of the problem. Flashing lights from a patrol car marked an accident on the side of the road, and a firetruck blocked the two left lanes. Beyond that, cars finally thinned out as they accelerated to make up lost time. Alex spotted an opening and took it.

She immediately discovered why traffic had avoided that particular path. Unsecure debris from the accident littered the road, and she plowed right over it. A mile or so later, her car lurched and pulled to one side. "Not good," Alex muttered as she eased to the left shoulder of the interstate.

After rolling to a stop, Alex flicked on her hazard lights

and drew three deep breaths. Thanks to her, oncoming traffic had already slowed again.

Bracing herself, she jumped out and inspected a flat tire on the front passenger side. Her stomach twisted. *And no phone.* She wouldn't be able to call for roadside assistance. Worse, she wouldn't be able to alert Hope to her situation.

Alex sucked in air flavored with car emission and blew it out raspberry style. She'd have to change the tire herself. Thanks to Dad, she carried a spare and a tool kit, both tucked away in a well in the trunk and secured with a bolt and wing-nut fastener.

By the time she dragged out six bottles of laundry detergent she'd bought at Costco and a gym bag stuffed with dirty clothes she'd stashed in the trunk, sweat beaded on the back of her neck. The Texas heat showed no mercy, no matter what time of year it was. "Whoever designed this emergency set up was an idiot," Alex mumbled as she peeled back the black lining.

She fitted the car jack under the frame. Now all she had to do was turn the crank, and the gadget could lift her car high enough to pull off the tire and replace it.

Three minutes later, Alex threw her hands in the air. The car was no higher off the ground than a bulldozed snail, and she was crankier than the slow-working crank. *Now what?* Some of the emergency vehicles from the accident down the road had to pass her by on their way home. Surely one of them would stop and render aid. She would simply wait. With her taser. Just in case.

The guardrail offered a front row seat to her disaster, and she took it. Trying to quell the bubbling unrest that threatened to consume her, Alex scanned the horizon. Above the stretch of road, the sky pinked at the edges. Sunset would be close behind. Not good.

The purr of a muscle car caught her attention. A

vehicle slowed behind her on the shoulder. It was the green Mustang, the one she'd cut off trying to escape the traffic jam. Goosebumps rose on Alex's arms, and she pulled the taser out of her pocket. That driver—a male, it seemed—should have been well past her by now. She thumped the stun gun against her leg, weighing her options. Should she threaten her would-be angel? Or welcome him? *Maybe it's someone who doesn't hold grudges and knows how to change a tire.*

Besides gifting her with a taser, her father had drilled the habit of memorizing physical details should she ever need to file a police report—as if he expected she'd be single for a long time and needed to protect herself. Still, the pounding of her heart probably wasn't due to fear, but the fact that the man who climbed from the Mustang was hot, and not in a Texas-heat kind of way.

He stood perhaps 6'2" and appeared to be around thirty years old. His mop of dark ginger hair stood out like a rogue leprechaun. *Close to a L'Oréal auburn.* Which went to show, she supposed, that when it came to describing someone, sometimes flipping through hairstyle magazines paid off.

He wore unassuming jeans and a classic green button-down shirt. Not the cheap fifteen-dollar Amazon sort, but a tailored $150 one from Neiman Marcus. He held a Whataburger soda, proof he must have stopped, and giving him an alibi for showing up now instead of passing her on the highway earlier. So not your typical highway robber, and cuter than a whole litter of golden retrievers.

"Hello, AK 622," he said, cheeks dimpling into a smile. "Need some help?"

Alex crinkled her nose. "AK 622?"

Stepping closer, he gestured at her tailgate. "Your license plate number. Unless you have a name?"

Red flags popped up in Alex's mind. The charm. The friendliness. Oh, he was smooth. Still—

"Alexandra." She shrugged, feigning a calm that didn't touch her veins. "My friends call me Alex."

"I'm Patrick." He reached out his hand as if expecting an old-fashioned handshake.

Alex ignored the offering, giving an awkward "Hello" wave instead.

Brows lifted, he let his arm drop. "What seems to be the problem, Alexandra?"

She shifted her gaze to his, determined to measure his mettle. A whiff of fresh sea scent caught her—the magic of an expensive cologne, perhaps. One side of Patrick's mouth curled upward, and her stomach quivered, whether from mistrust or interest, she couldn't tell. Alex swallowed hard and shook her head to clear it.

"A flat tire, obviously." She pointed to the jack. "And I don't seem to have the right coordination to work this darn contraption."

Patrick squatted next to the offending tire. "I can change that for you."

"I'm fine, don't worry about it." How many times had she heard on the news about a good Samaritan getting hit by a passing car when they stopped to help a stranded traveler? She couldn't have his death on her conscience. She cleared her throat. "But you can call roadside assistance for me."

His eyes narrowed. "Why don't you call?"

"I left my phone at home."

A sudden laugh burst from Patrick. "You're not very lucky, are you?"

So he puzzled out her secret anyway. Guilty relief flooded her. "No, I'm not lucky at all. But I'd count it fortunate if you could make that call for me."

Still smiling, Patrick pulled his cell phone from his

back pocket and typed in a number. He dictated details, sweeping the area with a quick glance before clicking off. "Done. Anyone else you need to notify?"

"My friend, Hope. I'm supposed to meet her for a St. Patrick's Day celebration. Can I text her?"

"Of course." He held out the phone. "I'm impressed you have her number memorized."

Alex slumped. "I don't. She's on speed-dial. So never mind." She blew out rough air and lowered herself toward the guardrail. She missed the edge and lost her balance, but Patrick caught her flailing arm and steadied her. "Thanks. I guess you can go now," she said, pulling free from his grip.

"I've got time. It's getting dark, and based on what I've seen, there's no telling what kind of trouble you might get into before help arrives."

Without permission, he settled on the steel perch next to her. But far enough away that she could execute a groin kick if things went south. He put both hands on his knees, as if relaxing on a couch. The surrounding chaos didn't seem to faze him. In fact, he held himself with the easy confidence of someone who probably volunteered at a soup kitchen or tutored underprivileged kids.

Beyond his silhouette, the sky darkened, drawing twilight closer. Under different circumstances, one might even call it romantic ... if romance involved oil stains and questionable roadkill.

Make the best of it. "Do you have any plans for the evening?"

"Why?" His eyes widened. "Are you asking me out?"

Her face heated. The nerve of the guy! "No, I'm just being polite."

"Oh." He sagged.

Patrick's clear disappointment made Alex regret her callous tone. "Kidding. I'm kidding." She touched his knee to draw his attention. "I'm really glad you're on the road right now." She meant the words, and when his friendly smile returned, she warmed to it. "Do you have any St. Patrick's Day traditions?"

"I usually run the St. Paddy's Day 5K Dash, but not this year." He clenched his fingers, then rubbed them against his pant leg. "Got a big project I'm working on."

"But you still found time to help me," she pointed out.

He nodded in response. "There's always time to help others. Wait, does that sound lame?"

"Not at all. I bet old ladies worldwide are rejoicing at the prospect of your assistance across the street." Alex cocked her head. "Do you live in Dallas?"

"Yes. I have an apartment in Highland Park."

He said it casually, as if living in one the most expensive areas of the city was no big deal. Maybe he was lying to impress her. "Wow. You must have a good job to afford that."

"I do, in fact." He quirked a grin. "I'm a writer."

"Oh!" His answer caught her off-guard. She could see him as a smooth-talking lawyer, maybe. A pro-soccer player, likely. A mild-mannered doctor, plausible. But a writer? Alex laughed, imagining what kind of story he might cook up about rescuing a fair maiden from a flat tire. "I better be nice to you then. I've heard that if you anger a writer, they make you into a character in a book and kill you off."

His eyes danced. "Yep! But don't worry. I would never do that to a woman who wields a taser like a Samurai sword."

"What!" Alex tucked the weapon behind her back, then slapped on an exaggerated evil grin and brought it out again. She flicked the device on and pointed it at him.

Patrick raised his arms like a bandit caught by the sheriff. "Don't shoot! I'm innocent."

"That you are." She let it buzz with electricity, then lifted an eyebrow. "Sorry. Old habit. But you're safe. So far, I've only crackled the air to scare off a dog. And tasered myself. Accidentally."

"Ouch!" Lowering his arms, Patrick nodded toward her car. "Somehow I'm not surprised."

"I know, right? I'm a walking, talking mishap waiting to happen. But enough about me." She pressed her lips together. "You're kind of interesting. And a mystery. You say you're a writer. Except you're living in Highland Park. There's a little disconnect here. Writers typically don't make a lot of income unless they have a bestseller."

"You have a limited view of a writer." Patrick rubbed his chin. "We don't just write books because—well, you're right, there isn't always a lot of money in that. I write scripts for a video game production company. And since I'm Irish," he waved at his hair, as if that were his proof, "my latest saga is an adventure that takes place along the shores of the Emerald Isle. Honestly, that's one of the reasons I pulled over to help. The hair, the tough camo army shirt, the fierce look in your eyes—"

"That was natural frizz, lack of wardrobe choices, and earned frustration," Alex said.

Patrick chuckled, voice low and dry in his throat. "I guess irritation and determination share similar facial tics."

"Oh, now that's a hoot." Alex tucked a wayward strand of hair behind her ear. "Why is my look so important to a writer?"

He shrugged and leaned closer to her. "I'm trying to find the right description for my female lead. And you look the way I envisioned Kiara, my warrior, would look. When I spotted you roadside, you took my breath away."

"Very poetic. Most people call that asthma," she quipped.

"No, really." Patrick raised a finger, cutting off her objection. "I had to stop. Drink in all the details of your face so I could remember you when I went to work tomorrow."

"Me?" Alex frowned. "I look like a warrior princess?"

"You don't know how to take a compliment, do you? Yes, you've got the physique of a beautiful and fierce-looking warrior. And once we hire a new digital artist, he can take my description of you and add a simple silver helmet, engraved with Ireland's Yellow Furze, on top of that hair." Patrick reached out and brushed her chin with his thumb. "Add green war paint on the cheeks, brown to highlight the eyes—" He stopped abruptly. His face drained of color, and he looked away. "Sorry. That sounds creepy. I should go."

Alex grabbed his arm. "Wait. You said your company is hiring a digital artist?"

"Yes. Our last one quit. Cited *creative differences* because I complained about how he made all my female characters look so ..." Patrick frowned.

"So what?" Alex prompted.

"Busty."

Alex stifled a giggle, and Patrick lifted his hands, palms up.

"His images detracted from my storyline," he said. "I want my stuff to be more kid friendly. It's a bigger market because the teens will still purchase the game without sexualized characters, and parents of the younger audience will buy in too."

Could she be so lucky? Well, not lucky that he wouldn't classify her as busty, because no one brags about wearing a padded size B bra, but lucky that he needed someone with her qualifications. Alex pulled her shoulders back. "How can I apply to work at your company?"

"We don't hire models."

A model? She laughed. "No. I could be your new digital artist."

"Get out!" Patrick's jaw dropped. "That's really your job?"

"Well, no. Not yet." Alex bit her lip. "But I got my degree in graphic design, and I have a portfolio you can look at." Sudden realization burst her bubble. "If I had my phone. Which, unfortunately, I don't." She snapped her fingers. "But I posted some images on my Instagram account. Look me up."

Patrick fumbled with his phone and handed it to her. "You'll find it faster than me."

Nodding, Alex clicked the app and pulled up her profile. "You're lucky my father convinced me to make a business profile so I could someday use it for marketing. Some of the images are my attempts at cute clipart. And the seasonal ones are my way of celebrating the holiday without much effort. You'll have to wade through the weird quotes or poems I posted. Look for characters I made—celebrities I put into cartoon form and more complex fantasy characters that might fit your needs. I guess my profile is kind of a mishmash of all the things I love. I probably should have branded more. Anyway, here."

She shoved the phone into his hands. It lit up Patrick's face as he scrolled through her feed. Her muscles tensed when he paused or grunted in reaction to the images. Did he like them? Or not?

The longer he took, the further her heart sank. Purple velvet now kissed the distant skyline, and a glow rose from the buildings. How much time did it take to go through someone's social media account anyway?

Alex finally tired of counting cars with a headlight out and shifted her gaze to Patrick. Who was she kidding? She was Ms. Friday the Thirteenth, the bearer of bad luck, the woman with the cursed touch. And he was the spitting image of a Celtic deity, the luck of the Irish, Saint Patrick himself.

His phone rang, breaking her trance.

"Hello?" Confusion raced across his face. "No, I said the north tollway, not the south. What mile marker are you at? It's going to be pitch dark in twenty minutes. Never mind. We'll handle it here."

Oh, no. People like her didn't get breaks. They broke things. "That was road assistance, wasn't it?" she asked.

He nodded.

"Let me guess." She ticked off her predictions on three fingers. "They misunderstood your directions and took the wrong route. And now I'm stuck."

"Yes. But actually, you're not stuck." Patrick pocketed his phone and stood. "If I hire you, would you trust me enough to change your tire?"

"What?" Alex blinked. "You mean—*what?*"

"Alexandra, I want you to work for me." Patrick's Irish eyes smiled, flickers of light in the darkness. "You've got talent. Those fantasy images were spot on. Original, but still genre-specific. And I love your personality. Your sense of humor shines through everything. Even in the face of disappointment and heartache, you always posted words and pictures that were encouraging and uplifting. You fall down and get back up again. I like that determination. You seem like someone I could work closely with for a long time."

"A long time? But you can't just hire me off the streets." She waved her hands at the passing cars. "And I mean literally, off the streets. Can you?"

"Well, I know the boss personally—he's my dad." He lifted an eyebrow and handed her a business card. "You might have seen him in the news. Owner of the Flixar company."

Flixar? The biggest video company in the Southwest?

Gaping, she looked from the card to his face, but nothing came out of her mouth.

Leaning in, Patrick nudged her. "So what do you say?"

"I say my luck is changing!" Alex beamed at him.

"Changing?" Patrick released a puff of air, his breath cool on her skin. "Your luck is right where it needs to be. Don't you read your own posts? You broke your wrist but met your friend Hope in the hospital. You lost the house rental you wanted, but ended up in an apartment, which saved you enough money to buy that pricey iPad Pro you wanted for your digital work. When your heart got broken half-a-dozen times, you encouraged your followers. You misinterpreted a class syllabus, but it led to new curriculum guidelines. And if you hadn't gotten a flat tire on your way to an Irish pub to celebrate St. Patrick's Day with your friend Hope, you never would have landed your dream job at *Flixar*."

"I never thought of it that way." Alex ran her finger over the card.

"Sometimes, a new perspective is all it takes to recognize just how lucky you are that things don't go the way you plan, Alex."

She could have kissed him right then and there. "Alex, huh? What my friends call me. From some guy I just met."

"Alex." He winked. "From some guy who wants your phone number so we can meet again."

APRIL

♥ ♥ ♥

A PILGRIMAGE INTO PROMISE

FELICIA FERGUSON

MUD RELEASED JESSIE CAVANAUGH'S HIKING BOOTS WITH a slobbery *pop* as she eased onto a fallen cypress tree on the lake's grassy edge. Sunlight filtered through the canopy of oaks and pines, dappling the saw palmettos with brushes of greenish-gold. She took a deep breath of the soggy air and held it just for a moment, savoring the hints of jasmine from the vines that clung to trees further up the trail.

A woodpecker cocked his head, eyeing her from his perch on a broken tree limb jutting out of the murky water. After a heartbeat of wary consideration, he returned to pecking the decaying wood in search of lunch. A slight breeze lifted the sweat-soaked tendrils of hair that had escaped her ponytail, sending a chill across her skin. She smiled despite the sensation, grateful for the luscious break from the sodden air.

As an eco-tourist guide, she was accustomed to bears, birds, and bugs, but Florida's humidity was a different beast altogether. Even in mid-April, the swampy forest air was as soaked as the moss. Jessie pulled the elastic hairband from around her dark hair and wove the freshly-freed locks into a tight braid. Maybe that would keep the humidity from teasing it loose again.

Swiping her arm across her forehead, she wondered for the hundredth time how on earth she'd allowed her sister, Maggie, to guilt her into this trip. Then she glanced over at Willie, and she remembered. Again.

Willie, Jessie's fifteen-year-old niece, had been begging her dad, Joe, to take her on the annual Pascua Florida Pilgrimage for the last two years. This year, he'd finally agreed she was ready for the rough terrain, but then Joe, an Army Ranger, had gotten a temporary duty assignment out-of-state. Maggie, accustomed to playing both mom and dad when needed, had stepped up and said she would still take Willie. But then Maggie broke her ankle while paddleboarding last week.

When Jessie got the call about both the ankle and the trip, she had backpedaled as fast as she could. It wasn't just an eco-tour commemorating Ponce de León's discovery of Florida. This was a true church pilgrimage to honor the Spanish missionaries who accompanied de León and planted the first cross on the Floridian shores.

Once she'd turned eighteen and was out from under Mom's attendance requirements, Jessie had bid church goodbye. She had other priorities for her time and interests. Maggie, however, had remained wholeheartedly devoted after she went to college, even converting to Catholicism when she married Joe.

Out of family obligation, Jessie attended their wedding,

Willie's christening, and even her confirmation two years ago. But wasn't taking Willie on this God-trek a bit much to ask? She was no spiritual mentor. Jessie had even tried to use their religion as an excuse. "But I'm not Catholic," she had protested. To which Maggie replied, "It's not a Catholic-only event. It's open to people of all faiths—even those with only a little."

There was no getting out of the trip. And really on some level she was happy to go. After all, nature was her first love, and enjoying a different aspect of it would be enlightening. She'd just about reached her customary level of excitement for planning an excursion when Maggie laid out her final rationale. "And who knows, maybe you'll finally meet someone."

"Don't start," Jessie had cautioned as a shiver slipped over her heart. "You know me. My life, my work, it's everything I've ever wanted. A dream come true."

Maggie had looked doubtful—much as she always did whenever the topic of Jessie's singlehood came up. "But what good is a dream if you don't have someone to dream with you?"

"This seat taken?"

Jerked from her memories, Jessie wiped her brow again and shifted her Costa sunglasses to try and make out the form hidden in the sun's glare. Marcus Tannenbaum. Oh.

She smothered her sigh and waved him to the spot next to her, a few feet away from Willie and the two teenage boys Marcus was leading through the pilgrimage. A water bottle dripping with its own sweat hovered in her view. Well, at least he was good for something other than corralling teenagers and twinning with Ryan Gosling.

"Jessie, right? You're Willie's aunt."

Jessie took a long, slow swig of the water bottle and nodded.

He stuck out a hand and grinned at full wattage, making

him even easier on the eyes. "Marcus. I'm from Santa Rosa Beach. Between Destin and Panama City. You?"

She released his hand and gave him a half-hearted shrug. "North Carolina. A map dot you wouldn't know. But Willie's from Savannah."

"How did you hear about the pilgrimage?"

"By accident. Literally." She gave him a brief overview of the events.

"Oh, I'm sorry." Concern darkened his eyes before he flicked a glance in Willie's direction. "She hasn't said anything about that."

"It's life. And life in the military," Jessie said as her lips flinched with resignation. "Willie was devastated. So I stepped in."

"Even though it's not about the faith for you?"

Jessie's head snapped back, eyes locking onto his. Was there judgment in his question? Only friendly curiosity lurked in his gaze. "How did you know?"

Marcus shrugged. "Just a guess."

Her lips flattened as her eyes darted to Willie. "What did she say?"

Marcus flashed a soothing smile. "Don't worry. Nothing bad. Or even all that revealing. She's pretty tight-lipped when you get right down to it. I was just able to add up the details." He leaned toward Jessie, and his voice dropped to a conspiratorial whisper, "I was pretty good at math in school."

A grin crawled up her cheeks and, helpless to stop it, Jessie shook her head. *So not only is he easy on the eyes, he's good for a joke too. Huh.*

"So an eco-tourist guide, huh? Pretty cool gig. What's your favorite location?"

Jessie wiped her brow then sipped from her water bottle. "I specialize in the Blue Ridge Mountains, so I'd guess you could say that's my favorite place."

Marcus nodded. "This must be like another day at the office to you, huh?"

Her eyes narrowed as she searched his face. *Was that a pick-up line?* His smile was open and friendly, and his brown eyes appeared intrigued. *Possibly.* She hugged the wariness closer as she took another draw of water. This was a get-in, get-out favor only. She liked her life as it was, free to come and go with no commitments to anyone but herself and the odd, passing nod to God.

However, something pinged her heart. From every indication, Marcus was a decent guy. He was a high school science teacher escorting two of his teenage students on the pilgrimage, and he seemed completely happy about the endeavor. And so far, every one of the church members on the trek had been welcoming and friendly.

He drank the rest of the water in his bottle in a few gulps, but that same patient curiosity lingered in his eyes.

Jessie's stomach unclenched. "Well, I've always loved the outdoors. Especially the mountains. Mom used to say I'd rather sleep in a tent in the backyard than in my own bed. But I guess, I don't know. Something about nature just calls to me. I feel centered, at peace, when I'm out here."

Marcus nodded but said nothing as he surveyed the grassy landscape that edged the wide, wild lake. After a few minutes in silence, he glanced over at her. "I get it."

He must have read her disbelief because he spread his hands in a helpless gesture as a self-deprecating smile twisted his lips. "What? I do. I've always been more comfortable outdoors than in. Something about the openness, the air ... maybe even the possibilities."

Jessie's eyes met his, weighing the truth of his words. She wanted to doubt him, but as she absorbed his quiet, sincere tone and warming gaze, she couldn't.

He knew. He understood.

The warmth in his eyes deepened into intrigue and interest. She licked her lips as her pulse skipped. *Okay, time to cut bait.* Grabbing the cap from her water bottle, she screwed it into place and flicked him a quick smile. "Probably should be heading back to the group."

Marcus watched her then nodded. But the light in his eyes didn't change. He rose and extended his hand. "Ladies first."

♥ ♥ ♥

Jessie intrigued Marcus. Okay, more than intrigued him. He watched her loosening braid swing against her shoulders as she and Willie trudged through the grassy trail up ahead of him and the boys. Like her, the braid was no-nonsense, but unable to resist the draw of its surroundings. She ran her fingers through the drooping strands, then tucked them behind her ear.

When he'd prepared to lead Josh and Danny on the pilgrimage, he'd had the oddest sense the trip was about more than encouraging their faith and interest in the Florida outdoors. Was it possible that "more" had something to do with Jessie?

He couldn't deny she was beautiful. Her dark hair, amber-colored eyes, and slightly upturned nose had captured his attention from the moment she'd stepped into the group orientation meeting. Living and working in a resort area, however, he'd seen his share of beautiful women. Whatever attracted him to her had to be more than physical.

Maybe it was their shared love of the outdoors? The recognition that they each possessed a restlessness that only nature could soothe?

He sighed and shook his head. Jessie lived and worked hundreds of miles away. And besides, he got the distinct feeling that the last souvenir she wanted from this trip was a man. He tugged his gaze from her and turned his attention back to the boys. They were why he was here. Not some passing interest that had nowhere to go. "Guys, how are you doing? Feet still okay? Do I need to break out the moleskin yet?"

♥ ♥ ♥

Light from the Coleman oil lamp flickered against the canvas of the tent, tempting Jessie to make shadow figures with her hands, but she smothered the idea. Willie was fifteen, not five.

Willie tucked her lower lip between her teeth as she studied the ceiling. Jessie had watched her during the service and campfire singing. Willie recited prayers and sang along with the rest of the group, but she seemed distracted. Jessie had chalked Willie's lack of enthusiasm up to first-day fatigue, maybe even missing Joe and Maggie and decided to leave Willie to her thoughts.

In truth, Jessie really wasn't sure how to get her to talk anyway. As much as she loved Willie, their locations and Jessie's work didn't allow for much one-on-one time, even at family holiday events. And teen years were always rife with melancholy—at least Jessie's had been.

"I saw you talking with Marcus Tannenbaum earlier today." Willie's soft voice, laden with interest beyond her years, pierced the nighttime birdsong.

Not you too. Jessie met Willie's gaze and shook her head. "Just idle talk."

Willie picked at a loose thread in her sleeping bag, her eyes flicking back and forth from Jessie to the fabric. "Josh and Danny really like him. Said he's a good guy. Great teacher and easy to talk to. They all go to the same church too."

Jessie nodded. This was a rhetorical conversation, wasn't it?

Willie turned on her side and fiddled with the zipper of her sleeping bag, drawing it up and lowering it. Her gaze once again flicked from the bag to Jessie.

Jessie cut off any further forays into the topic of Marcus. "You're missing your dad, aren't you?"

Willie shrugged, then paused her fidgeting to study the lamp light. "It's not like he could say no to orders. Much as I sometimes wish he could."

Having no answer for the realities of military life, Jessie held her tongue and hoped the quiet would lull Willie to sleep.

But a few minutes later, she asked, "Do you ever get that feeling that there's something much bigger than you when you're out here?"

Jessie swallowed her sigh. What was it about the night and the quiet that led people to such philosophical conversations? Deciding to defuse her growing discomfort with Willie's choices of topics, Jessie teased, "You mean like a black bear?"

Willie shook her head and punched Jessie lightly in the arm. "No, Aunt Jessie, something you can't see, but you can still feel."

As much as she could put off Willie's interest in her personal life, Jessie couldn't deny Willie was right about the sensation. It was almost exactly what she'd told Marcus earlier. "Yeah, I get that feeling."

"What do you think it is?"

Jessie sighed and stared at the tent's ceiling. "To be honest, I really don't know." But based on Marcus's earlier contemplations when they sat together on the fallen tree, she had the disconcerting feeling he might know. He might even feel what she felt.

Shaking off the sensation, Jessie reached over and

dimmed the lantern. "Get some sleep. We've got a long canoe trip and hike tomorrow."

But despite her advice to Willie, Jessie still didn't close her own eyes for another few hours. Marcus and their earlier conversation rolled around in her heart. By the time she finally managed to fall asleep, the roiling thoughts merged into a single question—*Maggie, were you right about me meeting someone here?*

♥ ♥ ♥

While Willie finished breakfast with Danny and Josh, Jessie packed up their tent and supplies, unable to shake the question that lingered in her dreams. She slung their sleeping bags and the tent into the bed of the truck that would meet them at the next campsite. Dusting her hands, she surveyed the selection of canoes for the first part of the day's trek. She and Willie would have a two-seater, and Jessie couldn't help but wonder what the day's conversation might bring, given Willie's searching questions the previous night.

"Ready for day two?"

Jessie jumped as Marcus's voice jerked her from her ponderings. Her pulse skipped and heat stole up her cheeks as she turned to find his chagrined smile accompanied by an apologetic gaze. Hoping he'd dismiss her blush as a reaction to the warming air, she shrugged. "Yes. It's not my favorite. I actually prefer kayaks, but when in Rome, right?"

"Right." Marcus glanced back at the rest of the group, then lowered his voice. "Hey, about yesterday. I didn't mean to put you on the spot. You know, asking about your work and why you love it. Nature, the outdoors, it's just a subject that's near and dear, so ..."

Jessie nodded as she tucked her hands into the pockets

of her cargo shorts. "No, I get it. Willie mentioned you were a science teacher, yeah?"

Marcus nodded and leaned against the truck. His gaze drifted to the trees that edged the campground. "Botany major in college. My parents were missionaries in Peru, and I was fascinated by the rainforests when I was growing up. Was sure as soon as I graduated, I'd head out into the jungle and discover a rare plant species."

Jessie caught the wistful tone in his voice and, hoping to ease it, flashed a teasing grin. "I've heard teaching is a jungle of its own."

Marcus chuckled, then sobered. He propped an elbow against the truck bed as he continued to study the woods. "Yeah, and sometimes dreams don't come true."

Jessie's heart clenched. Her lips turning down, she squeezed his forearm. "Maybe, and maybe sometimes you just need someone to dream with."

Marcus's gaze met hers, and shivers skimmed the back of her neck. She swallowed hard, trying to wet her suddenly dry mouth. Her thoughts stuttered, then slammed into high gear as she watched something more than interest flash in his eyes. *Why did I just say that? Maggie, you need to get out of my head right now!*

She took a step back and crossed her arms, running her hands over her skin and soothing the prickling sensation. "I—ah. I ... need to go ... uh ... check on Willie."

She flicked her lips into what she hoped was something resembling a smile, then darted over to the breakfast area, glomming onto Willie and the boys and diving deep into a discussion of the day's trek. But she couldn't shake the sensation or Maggie's earlier words.

Was Marcus someone she could dream with?

♥ ♥ ♥

Marcus swallowed his shock—or, at least, he hoped he did. Being a teacher meant getting all sorts of random and often probing questions. But Jessie's words, coupled with the raw but reluctant interest lurking in her gaze, hit him right in the gut.

He'd fallen asleep last night and dreamed of Jessie's reluctant smiles and amber eyes. But when his heart somersaulted at seeing her in the breakfast line, he'd admitted his attraction was much more than physical. Something deeper drew him to her.

And then there was whatever just happened between them. That sudden insight, that knowing, that had popped between them like a summer rainstorm in the Panhandle, quick, drenching, but gone almost as soon as it arrived.

Marcus studied her as she talked with the kids, his mind faithfully replaying her words. Words that even she seemed to be stunned she had said. Was she right? Were his dreams, now long dormant, still attainable if they were shared with someone? And could that someone possibly be her?

Much as they loved him, his parents had never really understood his draw to the jungle. In truth, he didn't fully understand it either. He just simply knew that was where he was meant to be. While they supported his choice of a major, Dad had insisted he get a degree he could definitely use. Since Marcus had grown up working with kids, he figured teaching was the best option. But while working with kids and hiking the forests and woods around the Florida panhandle were fulfilling, Marcus had never gotten past the draw to the rainforest.

But here was Jessie, who had known him less than twenty-four hours, and she understood. She felt the call herself.

His gaze caught on the other pilgrims as they gathered for the morning service. While neither he nor the boys were Catholic, he made a point of attending the Latin services out of respect for the pilgrimage.

He whistled toward Josh and Danny who were in deep discussion with Willie and Jessie. "Hey, guys! Looks like they're about ready to start." The boys scrambled to their feet, Willie joining them. But Jessie remained where she was. He flicked a quick, questioning glance back to her, then asked, "You coming?"

Her brow wrinkled a moment, then a light flickered in her eyes. "Why not?"

♥ ♥ ♥

Since the service was conducted in Latin, and Jessie had only a passing familiarity with it—and that based solely on her study of flora and fauna—she let her thoughts drift. What would it be like to share her love of the outdoors, her joy at discovering hidden jewels in nature, with someone? With Marcus?

Their eyes met above the heads of their charges, and Jessie glanced quickly away. He was definitely interested. And interesting. But was she? She'd told Maggie the truth. She did love her life. Enjoyed being single. The freedom, the flexibility to go anywhere and do anything—even at the drop of a hat.

But there was still that niggling thought, the possibility of shared dreams. And seeing those mutual dreams become reality.

By the time the priest said the only word Jessie recognized, curiosity, and even a bit of wonder, had softened her heart, opening it to truly consider Maggie's words.

Willie squeezed her arm, pulling Jessie from her thoughts. "I'm going to take a look at the canoes. Maybe we get to pick our own?"

Jessie smiled and waved her on, noticing Willie did

more than peruse the watercraft options. She met Josh near a long, red fiberglass canoe, her lips lifting in a shy but attentive smile. Jessie shook her head.

"Don't worry," Marcus said as he joined her. "Josh is more interested in trail biking and skimboarding than girls right now."

Jessie squelched her startle. She really needed to put a bell around Marcus's neck. "Ah, I wasn't worried. Too much distance anyway."

"You think so?"

Something flashed in Marcus's eyes, and Jessie had the oddest sensation he meant for people other than Josh and Willie. A smile crept up her lips as her heart flip-flopped. Something whispered inside her. *Take a chance.* She took in a quick fortifying breath and added, "Well, for them anyway. Adults have a bit more flexibility."

His cheeks curved as his eyes lit up with something like hope. Jessie couldn't help but reach for his hand. She gave it a long squeeze and nodded. *Okay, let's give this a shot.*

She turned her eyes to the woods and water ahead of them and asked, "What do you see out there?"

Marcus rubbed his thumb across the back of her hand as peace seemed to steal over him. He studied the vista, then turned his gaze to hers. His eyes glowed with promise. "Dreams waiting to be achieved."

Jessie's lips lifted in a wide smile. "Yeah, me too." She squeezed his hand once more, then released it. "Let's go get them."

MAY

♥ ♥ ♥

A RUN FOR REDEMPTION

FELICIA FERGUSON

LADIES IN WIDE-BRIMMED STRAW HATS SIPPED MINT JULEPS and mingled with men clad in pastel shirts and bow ties.

The race announcer's mechanical voice barely dented the conversations about stables, horses, and jockeys. The sweet scent of bourbon and fresh mint wafted on the early May breeze. Jim Green swallowed, clenching his trembling hands. He'd given the alcohol up. For Cobalt Night. And despite the craving that ate at him, he wasn't about to go back on a promise.

Now if Cobie could just keep her end of the bargain and win the Kentucky Derby.

The strains of "My Old Kentucky Home" wept from the marching band. As a lifelong Kentuckian, Jim readily added his voice to the crowd, singing lyrics that cried of longing and loyalty to the home state. As they entered the chorus, he craned his neck to watch the field of horses parade to the track before finally spotting Cobalt Night and Rico, her jockey. "There's my girl."

Moments later, the bugler rallied the crowd with his call to the post. The air thickened with anticipation as the horses loaded into the starting gates. Twenty-one racers in the field, and Cobalt Night was smack dab in the middle of both the gates and the rankings.

With a crash, the gates flew open. The crowd roared, and Cobalt Night took the lead early. By the quarter turn, she was a half-length ahead of her nearest rival.

Heart pounding in his ears, Jim clenched his fists. *Come on, Cobie.*

At the half turn, Cobie was a full length ahead and pulling away. Jim's hopes soared as tears of joy blurred the track. She would do it. She would wear the rose garland in the winner's circle. And he would crawl completely out of the hole he'd dug for himself.

But then ... Cobie stumbled.

Jim's breath froze as Rico flew over her head and onto the dusty track. Riders swerved and careened, barely avoiding him and the horse. Jim should have worried about Rico, but his eyes remained on Cobie as she struggled to a stand.

"Get up, girl." His quiet urging was lost in the uproar of the crowd still engrossed in the race. "Come on, Cobie."

She finally rose, but the obvious favoring of her front right leg turned his stomach.

In the corner of his eye, someone pushed through the crowd toward him. Bill Corbitt. Jim tore his gaze from Cobie and read the worry in Bill's eyes, certain the same look stared back. Rico limped over, silks stained with dirt, but otherwise unharmed. He reached for Cobie's reins and patted her neck as the emergency vets hurried to the track. Heart somewhere below his knees, Jim rushed to the track steward with Bill close on his heels.

♥ ♥ ♥

Pained disappointment leaked through Marta Quintero. As the ER vet on duty, she had hurried to the track, concerned Cobalt Night's injuries could be fatal. But as Marta began her evaluation, she heaved a thankful sigh. Looked like a cannon fracture—not a life-ending injury, although the mare's race career was now questionable.

"How is she?"

Marta blew her dark bangs out her eyes with an irritated huff. A man in a white Oxford and blue tie pushed between the race stewards. Another man, white hair perfectly combed and dressed in a seersucker suit, joined him. "Who are you?" she asked.

"Cobie's trainer, Jim Green, and this is Bill Corbitt, her owner."

She studied the two men, but the anxious gleam in Jim's gaze tugged at her heart. She pushed it aside. His concern seemed real, but in her experience, horse trainers were more focused on performance than partiality. "I'm Dr. Marta Quintero." She turned her gaze to Cobalt's Night's leg and sighed. "I can't be sure without X-rays or an ultrasound to determine the severity, but I'm calling it a cannon fracture."

Marta's eyes narrowed as Jim paled. *It might not be a fatal injury for the horse, but it must be for him.* Empathy flickered through her as she surveyed the trainer. He plopped on the ground next to the mare. Shaggy blond hair, off-the-rack Target dress shirt, and khaki pants likely from the same shopping trip. He wasn't the typical race trainer. No, he was a man barely afloat, and he'd just lost his life preserver.

Marta pulled a syringe and glass vial of pain meds out of her kit. She broke the seal on the vial with the needle and pulled back the plunger. She ran a soothing hand along Cobie's neck, then slipped the needle under her skin, praying for quick relief. A few minutes later, Cobie let out a huge sigh and dropped her head into Jim's hands. He stroked her cheeks under the bridle and closed his eyes. Marta's lips lifted at the sweet sight. *Well, well. Looks like love to me.*

She made quick work of splinting Cobie's leg and wrapped it in hot pink vet wrap. The vet techs removed the saddle, handing it to the jockey who had just limped over to the owner. Bill laid a steady hand on the jockey's shoulder, and Marta smiled again, savoring the rare moment of acceptance instead of blame on the track. It truly had been an accident. She patted Jim on the arm, pulling his attention from the horse. "Let's get her off the track and get a better idea of what's going on."

♥ ♥ ♥

Six weeks later, Jim tossed a few flakes of grass hay into the rack in Cobie's stall. She shuffled through the thick bed of cedar shavings, gave the empty grain bucket a longing sniff, then turned to the hay.

"I know, girl. But with you confined to quarters, we can't give you too much food."

Bill joined him at the stall and watched Cobie with the assessing eyes of a long-time stable owner. "Recovery will take a while."

She'd had surgery the day after the injury. At least it was a clean fracture that could be held in place with pins.

Jim nodded. "Yeah, racing season is gone now. I'm sorry, Bill. I'll understand if you want to take her home."

Bill laid a supportive hand on Jim's shoulder and

smiled. "Vet'll be here any minute. Let's hear her thoughts before we head down any paths."

Jim glanced at his watch. It was odd that Dr. Quintero would keep a track horse on her caseload, but maybe Cobie had tugged on something in her like she had with Bill. And him. The crunch of tires on gravel pulled his attention from Cobie's contented munching. Jim turned and raised his hand, flagging down the new arrival.

"Morning, gentlemen. Good to see you again." Marta ducked her head in a quick nod and skirted around them, intent on her patient. Sliding the stall door open, she crooned to Cobie and held out her hand for the mare to sniff. Cobie chuffed, then returned to her hay.

Marta slid her hand down Cobie's leg, then paused. She glanced up at Jim. "I assume she's been confined since the race?" At Jim's silent nod, she asked, "How often have you been walking her?"

"Twice a day, ten to fifteen minutes at a time, starting two weeks ago, just like the surgeon prescribed."

"Good. Let's go ahead and get some new X-rays to check on how everything is healing up. But based on what I'm feeling and seeing, I'd say you can bump her to thirty minutes of walking twice a day for the next two weeks. If she handles that well, then turn her out in a small paddock on her own several times a day for about five minutes. I'll check her again ten weeks from now, and we'll talk about getting a rider on her."

"See? It's good news." Bill clapped Jim on the back as his cell phone rang. Unclipping it from his belt holder, he grimaced. "Gotta take this."

Marta slipped back out of the stall, returning with the portable X-ray machine, but Jim still felt her intrigued gaze as she worked. As their eyes finally met, he lifted his brows in a silent question.

Marta's cheeks pinked, and Jim couldn't help the

appreciative smile that slipped over his lips. Her dark hair and eyes and olive coloring made her more striking than pretty, but she was certainly beautiful.

She stepped away from Cobie and tapped a couple of buttons on the machine. "So I get the funny feeling Cobie isn't just a horse to you."

Jim shook his head and stroked Cobie's neck as Marta reset the machine to capture a different view. "When my wife died in a car wreck three years ago, I lost it. Hid in the bottle. Lost the string of horses I'd been training. Even on the edge of losing my house and the stable."

Marta's mouth dropped open, and she reached over to touch his shoulder. "I'm so sorry."

Jim nodded his thanks. "Bill and I have known each other for years—I started as a groom at his father's stables. Bill picked Cobie up at Tattersalls for pennies on the dollar. Said all the big-name trainers turned her down. Too scrawny. Wrong bloodlines. You name it, he heard it."

Marta clicked a few buttons as her lips lifted. "Closed doors are sometimes God's best directions."

Jim stared at her, reading in her eyes the story that lurked in her words, but let it be. "But Bill said he had a feeling about her, so he brought her to me. Then, he told me something I'll never forget." Jim fell silent as the memories crowded his mind.

"What was that?"

He blinked and refocused his eyes, finding Marta's curious, sympathetic gaze roaming his face.

"He said, 'Ginny would kill you for what you've done to yourself. If you want a shot at redemption, I think this horse is it. But it's your choice.'"

Marta picked up the equipment and moved to her truck to process the images. A few minutes later, she tapped on an iPad and pulled up the images. Bill leaned against the stall and, for the first time in years, prayed.

Marta returned with a pleased smile. "Everything's healing up nicely."

Bill's breath left him in a rush of relief. But even though the news was positive, Cobie's and his future remained nebulous.

"So what now?" Marta asked.

Jim blinked as Marta's question pierced his similar thoughts. "That's what I can't wrap my head around."

He turned back to the stall as Cobie eased over and sniffed his shirt pocket. He smiled and flashed a quick smile to Marta. "She's looking for peppermints."

Marta's lips lifted as she reached into her jeans pocket and joined him in the stall. She pulled out a red and white mint, unwrapped it, and held it flat in her outstretched hand. Cobie's ears pricked as she caught the scent, and she gobbled the candy down.

Marta gave her fond pat as Jim heaved a disappointed sigh. "Thankfully, she'll heal up in time, but by then all the big races will be run. My shot at getting my name back as a trainer is done. This looks like another closed door. For both of us."

Marta turned her gaze from Cobie to Jim, her eyes softening with sympathy even as her smile grew encouraging. "Lots of track-sore horses go into other sports. Looking at her confirmation and the way she runs, as long as the fracture continues to heal well, I think she'd make a great three-day eventer. It's not racing, but with careful training and monitoring the injury for arthritis, she could have a long and very successful career."

Jim shook his head. "That's true enough, but I don't know a thing about dressage or jumping."

Marta laid her hand on Jim's forearm and squeezed it. Her eyes brightened, and for the first time in weeks, tinges of hope bubbled in Jim's heart. "But I do. My dad trained some of the best three-day eventers when I was a teenager—one even went to the Olympics. And I rode every horse he trained. Still do, when I get time. I'll help you."

Disbelief warred with the burgeoning hope. Surely, she was joking. But as he continued to watch her, absorbing the steady certainty in her eyes and her offer, hope won out. Still, he had to know. "But why?"

Marta shrugged. "Let's just say I've got a soft spot for seeing the underdog make good." Cobie bumped Marta's hands and dropped her head. "And yeah, there's something about this horse." She gave Cobie's ears a gentle scratch and patted her neck before slipping back out of the stall.

As the sun caught her dark hair, Jim blinked. He wasn't sure he still believed in God, but if ever there were angels, Marta Quintero just might be one.

"So, what's the good word, Doc?" Bill asked as he ambled back to the stall, his gaze flicking between Marta and Jim.

Marta cleared her throat as her voice sharpened back to her professional tones. "X-rays look good. As long as she continues to behave on her restrictions, she should be back to training in about six or seven months."

Jim closed the stall door and tucked his hands in his pockets, his gaze flicking from Marta to Bill. "But the question is what type of training."

Bill's brow furrowed. "What do you mean?"

Jim tilted his head as doubt once more crept into his heart. He might be Cobie's trainer and love her like his own, but Bill still owned her. Marta's hand again squeezed his forearm in silent support. Jim took in a quick breath. "Marta wants to turn her into a three-day eventer since she's out of the big pay-off races. What do you think?"

Bill's eyebrows lifted in consideration as he shot a pointed look to Marta's hand where it rested on Jim's arm. His cheeks curved as intrigue flashed through his eyes. "She could still be your second chance."

Jim's cheeks heated at Bill's subtle hint, and his heart clenched. His gaze flicked to Marta, reading the warm empathy and feminine interest in her gaze. Bill was right, but was he ready to climb completely out of his hole and start a new life all around? Peace melted through him. *Yeah, I guess I am.*

Patting her hand, he turned back to Bill as hope took full root in his heart. "Okay, let's do this."

THE MEMORIAL

LORI Z. SCOTT

AMY STOPPED AT A SUPERSTORE AND PURCHASED A BOUquet of daisies for her father's grave. Not that her dad had been big on flowers, but the bright yellow petals reminded her of playing catch with him in the summer. She would work on her four-seam throwing grip and focus on trapping the ball in the glove without stinging her hand. Afterwards, they'd drink lemonade on the back porch and read jokes off the labels of the Laffy Taffy candies Dad always carried in his pocket. *How do you get an alien baby to sleep? You rocket. Why did the student eat his homework? His teacher said it was a piece of cake. When does it rain money? When there's a change in the weather*. Classic jokes, every single one.

Traffic picked up as Amy wove through the local college town where her dad used to work. The crowded streets didn't surprise her, considering the long holiday weekend. Neither did the brunch-time groups of students clustered on restaurant patios, flirting and sipping coffee. One brave soul planted a kiss on his partner's cheek.

Amy blew a raspberry with her lips and adjusted her rearview mirror to crop the couple out of her vision. Maybe someday she'd get swept away into light-hearted romance like that. Maybe she'd find someone like her dad. Smart. Kind. Athletic. Faith-filled. Devoted. Funny. But who was she kidding? With that lofty checklist, her dog Jeb was the closest thing she'd found to true love so far. The only thing the golden retriever truly lacked was intelligence.

And good hygiene.

And he wasn't such a good kisser either. Very slobbery.

"Face it, Amy, you need a human equivalent to Jeb," Amy muttered to herself.

New dormitory buildings and old brick classrooms gave way to open farm fields and pot-holed streets. Compared to the east side of the city, where she now lived, the houses were sparse and worn. She turned down a lonely road canopied by oak branches that led to the Meadows View Cemetery near the rural neighborhood where she grew up.

After parking next to a Chrysler Voyager with a handicapped sticker at the main entry, Amy paused to take a deep, cleansing breath. She had been only nine when a drunk driver hit her dad's car. It had been fifteen years since his death. Annual Memorial Day visits helped keep the memories from fading.

At first, Amy had argued with her mom about a May 30 pilgrimage. She'd sat through a lesson in her third-grade class and knew all the facts. The stubbornness of a child whose world no longer made sense bristled at the idea. "Memorial Day is supposed to honor our military service people who have died. Dad needs his own day."

Mom had countered with, "Well, your dad died on this day too, so the soldiers will have to share it."

In the end, Mom made a small concession and allowed Amy to take part in the National Moment of Remembrance at 3 p.m. From then on, Amy used that moment of silence to reflect in her own way.

Beside the daisies, her phone buzzed. Amy lifted it and pushed the speaker button.

"Did you make it okay?" Even over the airport background noise, her mom's voice betrayed an edge. No wonder, since a friend's wedding had called her out of town, preventing her from paying her respects along with Amy.

"No problems." Amy shut off the motor and pocketed the keys. "How about you? Do you board soon?"

"Not soon enough." Mom snorted. "You know I hate traveling alone."

"You hate doing anything alone." Amy smiled into the phone. "That's why you have me, remember?"

"Yes. Well." A brief silence betrayed her mom's anxiety. "Just be safe. Lock your doors. Don't talk to strangers. Don't stay out too late either. And drive slow."

"It's a fourteen-mile trip." Amy reached into the back seat and grabbed her silver sunshade. "And I know the way home, even in the dark. I'll be fine."

After five more minutes of assurances that yes, she'd water the plants and yes, she'd put the garbage out on Tuesday and yes, yes, yes to the rest of her mother's directions, Amy said goodbye and hung up.

Sighing, she bowed her head, soothing the beating of her heart. Lately, the pressure to conform to her mother's script for her life weighed heavy on her. Was it normal, the overbearing worry that made her mom want to dictate Amy's choices? Or the way Amy continuously bowed to her wishes?

As she climbed out of her Chevy, Amy's stomach

churned. *I love you, Mom. So. Much.* But Mom couldn't protect her from heartache forever. Someday, Amy needed a family of her own. Then maybe her mom could shift her worry to the grandkids.

Like every year, Amy pulled up her dad's photograph on her phone and blew him a kiss before taking the hike to the grave. Gravel crunched under her sneakers as she made her way past moss-covered mausoleums, concrete angels, and simple crosses. Her dad's granite headstone sat under a willow tree on the east end.

New buds peeked from the spring trees lining the iron fence. Pigeons cooed from the nooks and crannies of statues guarding the wealthier patrons. Water babbled from a fountain in the nearby pond. *Dad would have appreciated the peacefulness of his final resting place.*

Lost in her thoughts, Amy didn't notice her dad's grave already had two visitors until she bumped into them. Startled, she put a hand to her chest and caught her breath. She cleared her throat. "I'm sorry. I didn't see you there. Are you lost?"

A twenty-something-year-old Korean man turned in Amy's direction. He had dark hair, frosted at the tips in a K-Pop cut, dark eyes and dark lashes, but his smile seemed light and friendly. Straight-legged jeans and a crisp blue button-down shirt completed his look.

He had the hygiene factor down pat. Her dog Jeb might have met his match.

"We're in the correct spot. Right, *Appa?*" K-Pop crossed his arms and gave Amy the once over, as if she were the one out of place.

The older man, black hair graying at the temple, lifted his chin. "Of course." He had a deeper voice—perhaps he smoked, although she couldn't detect a sour odor—and tiny wrinkles around his mouth. Even though he appeared to be in his fifties, he leaned against a metal cane, the kind that folded up for easy carrying.

Frowning, Amy shook her head "No. This is my dad's grave." She laid the daisies at the headstone and traced the engraving with her finger. "See? Jack Beckman. I'm his daughter."

"Amy?" the older man said. "Amy Beckman?" He poked her arm with his cane. "I am Joon. And this is my son, Dal."

Despite his friendly demeanor, her mother's warnings about strangers hit Amy like ice. She took a step back, muscles tense. "How do you know my name?"

Smiling, the man rattled off a string of words Amy didn't understand.

Dal *tsked* and held up a hand. "In English, Appa."

"My apologies," Joon said, giving a slight bow. "I know your name because Professor Beckman talked about you all the time. I heard all sorts of stories about you making mud pies and drawing on the kitchen walls." Joon's English held a heavy accent, as if he had learned the language far after the cadences of another had embedded themselves in his mind. But his words held an earnest tone that reassured her. "And I loved every tale, because Professor Beckman was my hero." He paused, frowning. "I am sorry about your father's death, Miss Amy. I did not learn of it until I arrived on campus and tried to look him up."

"Hero? What do you mean?" she asked.

Joon shifted his stance. "When I first came to America as a graduate student, I was—" Joon cocked his head toward Dal. "How would you say it?"

"As confused as a wolf hunting for dinner in a chocolate bunny factory?" Dal quirked an eyebrow, his lips curling into a smile. "Or as confused as a mosquito in a wax museum?"

"No." Joon rolled his eyes. "I was as confused as an octopus swimming in a can of jelly. I knew English, but I didn't understand the culture. Fast food. Fast pace. Fast highs. Faster lows. So much pressure. Your dad was my physics professor, and when he noticed my—" He gestured at Dal. "What's the word?"

"Your bow tie? Your mismatched socks? Your charm?" Dal widened his eyes and shrugged.

Amy stifled a laugh. There was something precious and tender in their father-son banter. Something that found comfort in another person's quirks and strength in a shared bond. Something Jeb might offer if she scratched his belly just right, but that she hoped to find in a male that didn't bark and wag his tail.

Someone like Dal.

"Did he notice your Cliffs Notes?" she said, playing along. Dal winked at her, and her stomach fluttered.

"No." Joon pulled his lips in a straight line, but Amy swore the man grinned first. "My be-wildebeest."

"Bewilderment. But nice try." Dal slipped his hands into his pockets, a boyish gesture that made him a more appealing man in Amy's eyes.

"Fine." Joon rapped his cane against the ground. "When Jack Beckman noticed my bewilderment, he took me under his wing. Helped me navigate the curriculum. And campus life. And American cuisine. And American football. He even brought me to church and introduced me to the love of my life."

"Jesus?" Amy asked.

"Song Lee." Dal wiggled his eyebrows. "The most beautiful—"

"Cupcake? Vixen?" Joon clutched his chest. "Cherry blossom?"

Dal lowered his voice into a purr. "The most beautiful—"

He held Amy with an intense stare that dissolved into a playful grin. "*—mother* in the world."

Had he meant the compliment for her? Caught in his magnetic gaze, Amy's skin tingled, and her cheeks heated.

Dal let out a hiss of air, releasing his hold on her. "Sadly, Mom returned to Korea to care for my Nana and Poppy. So, for the past two days going on a week more, I got to—"

"Rock out?" Joon pumped his cane in the air. "Chew gum? Solve mysteries?"

"Entertain—" Dal swept his hand out. "—my father on my own."

"You can thank me later." Joon patted Dal on the cheek. "I will join my wife soon. I came for Dal's doctorate celebration, but the campus brought back so many happy memories, I extended my stay. Although I'd hoped to see Professor Beckman in better health. I believe he still owes me a game of chess. He last beat me after an adult Sunday School game night, and I called for a rematch. But he had to pick up his little girl from the pre-K room."

The hair on her arm stood on end. After the funeral, her mother didn't talk much about her dad. Amy figured she didn't want to relive the pain. But Joon had spent quality time with her father. He could fill the gaps in her memory. In her heart. "You visited my church. Did I ever meet you there?"

"No." Joon pursed his lips, giving him the comical look of a sleepy pug. "I met you—"

"At the laundromat washing your skivvies. In the grocery store buying Brussels sprouts?" Keeping a straight face, Dal gently elbowed Amy.

Amy's mind raced. "At *Cats,* the musical, singing 'Memories' from the lid of a trash can?"

"Good one," Dal whispered, and something warm bubbled in Amy's veins.

"I met you in the classroom." Joon's eyes lit up. "Advanced Classical Mechanics. You wore a layered yellow dress and long yellow gloves. I remember thinking, 'now there's a beautiful girl I'd like my son Dal to marry someday' and now, well, here you are without a ring on your finger but looking just as fresh and pretty."

Matchmaking? Amy shot Dal a look. A pre-arranged marriage to him might've been a bargain deal. "I remember that Halloween. I was five years old."

"That seems about right," Joon said. "You stood in the doorway like you were stuck in mud. But Professor Jack Beckman waved you forward and said something. What did he say?"

"'Peanut butter?' 'May the force be with you'?" Dal offered. "'I'm Batman'?"

"No." Amy's throat tightened. "He said, 'Don't be afraid. Come in.'"

"That's right!" Joon pointed at her. "And you marched right up to your dad and said, 'Trick or treat.' He gave you a big kiss and emptied a pocketful of Laffy Taffy into your pumpkin bucket." His gaze went out of focus, as if lost in the past. "I'd achieved half-a-dozen perfect test scores trying to impress the man, but I've never seen such a proud look on his face as the day you knocked on the door. Made me want to go out and buy a yellow costume for myself, just to show him how serious I was about my studies. What were you anyway? A talking banana? A stick of butter?"

Sudden longing swept through Amy, and she swallowed hard. Her words came out soft and choked. "I was—"

A sharp image of the classroom flooded her senses. Individual desks stood in neat rows. A musty smell tickled her nose. A dozen students turned their heads her way at her timid knock on the door. Her dad's familiar movement, pushing his glasses up the bridge of his nose to get a better look.

Dad. After he passed away, she had always stayed strong for her mother's sake. When was the last time she'd allowed herself to grieve? Amy's legs buckled.

Without hesitation, Dal slipped an arm around her waist and steadied her. "A princess? I bet you were a princess?" His tone had lost its light tease. Instead, it was laced with the same underlying concern she often heard in her mother's words. So he wasn't all humor. He had a serious side too. *Move over, Jeb.*

Blinking back tears, Amy nodded. "Yes. I was a princess. Belle, from *Beauty and the Beast.* My father danced with me. The night was magic."

Body trembling and strength plummeting, she leaned into Dal. Or melted might have been a better word, for she could no longer sense the boundary between where she ended and where he began.

As if acting on habit, he stroked the back of her hair.

His simple act of empathy calmed her. She drew in short breaths until the waves of sorrow passed. "I'm sorry. You must think I'm a fool. I hardly know you."

"It's okay." Dal gave one final squeeze before releasing her. "I recognize a wounded heart when I see one." His gaze briefly flicked to Joon before refocusing on Amy. "And I know a few tricks to mend them too. You want to go out for coffee? Talk?"

Amy hesitated. Her mom's voice screamed in her mind. *Just be safe. Drive slow. Lock your doors. Don't talk to strangers.*

But then, for the first time in a long time, she heard her father's voice whisper, *Don't be afraid.*

She straightened her back. "Yeah, I think I'd like that."

"Great!" Dal's quick nod sealed the deal. "I've got all afternoon. And I'm sure Joon has a ton more stories about

Professor Jack Beckman he'd like to share. And with you along, he'll have a doubly rapt audience. Right, Appa?"

Joon responded with a dry chuckle. "Did I tell you about the time I got my sines and cosines mixed up and the professor had to—how would you describe what happened?"

Dal raised a brow. "Give you a failing grade?"

The pug look returned to Joon's face. "Actually, yes." He clapped a hand on Amy's shoulder. "But also, Professor Beckman offered to tutor me. We met every Monday afternoon at the Boiler Café. I knew he had a busy schedule. But he also had, as he often said, a heart for the lost. Which, at the time, described me. Add overwhelmed and discouraged to the list, and it's a wonder I graduated at all."

"It's a wonder you can find your car keys on a regular basis," Dal said.

When Joon hefted his cane like a bat, Dal held up his hands in mock surrender. "Just kidding. You're the best, Appa."

Joon turned to Amy. "For old times' sake, why don't we go to the Boiler Café? I'll order you the best brew in town." Smirking, he added, "Dal's treat."

Amy laughed. "Sure. But I really prefer—"

"Cream and sugar?" Joon wrinkled his nose "Or that wimpy hazelnut flavor?"

"No." Amy lifted a finger. "Tea."

Twenty minutes later, an earthy but nutty scent greeted Amy at the door to the café. Cozy square and tall rounded tables sat snug around the room. Boilermaker pendants, football and basketball poster schedules, and glass-cased baseballs decorated the walls. The trio settled into a more secluded corner of the room, far enough away from the condiment station to avoid foot traffic but close enough to the front windows to get a view of the street.

Amy ordered cranberry herbal tea with a blueberry muffin while Joon and Dal ordered black coffee and bagels.

At first, Amy simply listened while Joon relayed stories about his conversations with her dad. But then she asked questions. If Amy teared up, Dal was always quick to add his humor in a way that eased the aching in her chest. How many times did she burst out laughing instead of exploding like a balloon thanks to Dal? She lost count.

A happy but oddly tight twist grew in Amy's stomach while Joon talked. It helped that Joon had a flair for storytelling. His animated face and steady pace held Amy's attention.

"I'll never forget trying to find the dining hall the first week. I didn't know where the cafeteria line formed, and I was too embarrassed to ask," Joon said. "I must have walked back and forth on the quad peeking in the front of every building a hundred times before Professor Beckman opened his office window and yelled, 'Joon. Stop!' He scared me to death, you know, this big booming voice coming out of the third story like a god. 'You look like a slow-motion bumper car,' he says. 'You stand right there. I'm coming to help you.' And then, my heart pounding like thunder, I just froze. Like this." Joon posed in a stance similar to a garden gnome. "And I didn't move. For probably five minutes, although it felt like five years. And then the professor comes running up, all out of breath because I guess he was afraid I'd wander off again, and ..."

As Amy listened, a sense of peace fell over her. This conversation, this father-son combo, felt safe. Loving. Their interactions were how visiting home during a holiday should be, minus the presence of one hairy dog at her feet. She relaxed, cupping the hot tea between her fingers, and drinking in the warm experience of this moment instead. The noise of customers talking and servers barking out orders and mugs clicking against the table faded bit by bit until all that remained was Joon's baritone voice, the tender attentiveness of Dal, and the ghost of her father's memory harmonizing with them all.

She jumped when an alarm went off on her phone. In a flash, reality crashed, and her contentment drained away. "I've got to go."

"Really?" Dal asked, disappointment evident in the way his lips turned down.

Pouty lips, quite kissable.

Amy shook her head, stuffing away that thought. Today was a chance meeting. A gift, really. But soon, Joon would return to Korea. And Dal would likely follow, even though he had indicated he had an engineering job at the local plant. Just like every other male relationship in her life except for Jeb, this bonding, or whatever enchantment you want to call what happened today, couldn't last. She'd been foolish to dream otherwise.

She stood to leave. "Yes. It's a tradition. Every Memorial Day at 3:00, I take a moment of silence to reflect."

"On what?" Dal turned his face upward, eyes tracking her movements.

"On death. On life." She frowned and reached for her purse. "On hopes for the future."

Dal rose next to her. "Isn't that what we just did for the last three hours?"

Schooling her face to hide her emotion, Amy scuffed her shoe against the floor. "Maybe. But this is something I need to do alone."

"No, you don't." Dal looked to Joon, who gave a quick nod. "We're here, reliving and mourning and celebrating your dad with you."

Her phone lit up, saving her from further comment. "My mom checking in," she said, flicking a trembling finger to open the message. She shifted her head back and forth, reading the text out loud. "3:00. I know it's your quiet time. I'm thinking of you. Be safe!" Her throat swelled, and she let her arm drop. "See? Tradition."

"Amy. Don't go. You're not alone." Dal inclined his head to the phone, using his hand to lift it to her face. "And maybe you never really were."

The letters blurred, and Amy wiped away a tear. He was right, in her heart she knew he was right. But this yearly ritual was a comfortable pain she nursed like a glass of wine at a cocktail party, and she wasn't sure if she was ready to give it up.

Still, Dal didn't waver. Even Joon had hefted himself to his unsteady feet and looked at her expectantly.

Darn. Sentimentality wasn't on her mental checklist.

Maybe the list needed adjusting.

"Okay." She sniffled. "So what now?"

"You stay right here with us ... with me ... for a little while longer. Maybe even meet me for lunch tomorrow without my elderly escort?" He grabbed her hand and rubbed his thumb over her skin. "I feel like I've known you all my life, even though it took twenty-seven years to meet you. And I hate to lose you now."

Like dangling on a precipice, Amy let the fire of Dal's touch hold her in place. She studied his face, searching for—

For what, exactly? For resolution of her past? For permission to pursue her own goals without Mom's direction?

Dal must have sensed her hesitation. "Running away when the clock strikes the hour is Cinderella's move. Belle took on a beast and tamed him. Isn't that why Amy's Halloween costume fit so perfectly, Appa?" Dal quirked a brow at the old man.

"Oh yes, absolutely." Joon pounded his cane on the floor. "Aw, you're breaking my heart. You know what you oughta do, Dal?"

"Tell Amy she's beautiful? Ask for her phone number?"

"Nah, kiss her, you idiot! How do you think I won Song Lee's heart? With my wit?"

Dal dropped her hand, as if embarrassed by Joon's outburst. "You see what he does to me?" He swept his arm toward Joon. "He's like a bowl of Ramen noodles."

Amy scrunched her nose. "What?"

"He's just a little over the top—" Dal slapped a hand against Joon's chest. "—but you still can't get enough of him."

Amy laughed. It was her dad's kind of humor.

Mental note. Jeb, you're now the number two creature I'd like to snuggle with tonight.

"We could catch a ball game." Dal pointed at a wall sports schedule. "There's a Memorial Day baseball tournament this weekend."

"I'd like that," Amy said. "Just let me text my mom first. I'm sure she's anxious for an update."

Her mother, in fact, had sent two more messages in the span of time it took Amy to accept Dal's invitation. *Did the visit go okay this morning? Did you remember to turn on the alarm when you left home?*

The visit was perfect, Amy texted. She paused, considering her next words. *And I remembered everything.*

After tucking her phone away, Amy hooked an arm through Dal's. All the way to the car, they traded banter about four-seam grips and fly balls. At the game, they made up fake histories for the players when their images flashed on the screen. Things like the first baseman is the love child of *Shrek* and Sonic the Hedgehog. They sang "Take Me Out to the Ballgame" like seals in a strainer. They predicted who would strike out. And they talked. And talked. And talked.

As days turned into weeks, the language of Amy's mom's texts changed from a list of reminders and cautions to things like, "The flowers Dal sent smell so good. Is he coming with us to church tomorrow?" Or, "I found your father's old baseball cap in the closet yesterday. He used to love that ratty old thing. Do you want it?"

Four months later, Joon and Song Lee flew back from Korea.

Upon their arrival, Dal presented Amy with a bag of Laffy Taffy and a diamond ring.

Jeb said yes for both of them with a sloppy kiss.

And the next Memorial Day, the newly formed family—all five and a half of them—six and a *half* if you included Jeb—put two dozen daisies on her father's grave.

GONE BUT NOT FORGOTTEN

FELICIA FERGUSON

"WELLS MONROE LEWIS, IT'S THE LAST DECORATION Day that will ever be held at your great-great-great grandparents's church. And you will come this year even if I have to drag you by the earlobe." Parker Fitzpatrick Lewis, my mama, had spoken. And, it would seem, so had my entire Fitzpatrick lineage.

I tried to swallow the ire bubbling in the back of my throat as I stared at Mama on the video call. Going back to River Fork United Methodist Church in Millwood, Alabama—a town that had neither a river nor a fork in it, mind you—remained right up there with jumping out of a perfectly good airplane on my bucket list of things *not* to do ever again in my life.

Mainly because both of those events coincided with

the presence of someone I never wanted to see again. John Mark Townsend. My childhood love, first kiss, and the man who jilted me at the altar two hours before our wedding.

Glancing at my office calendar, relief washed over me. I had one last card to play. And it was an ace. "Mama, the Southern Design Expo is that same weekend. You know how much business my firm gets from that event. I simply cannot go." I added a pleading bat of my eyelashes, certain that would sway her.

Mama's eyes narrowed as she weighed the excuse. "And where is it this year?"

Well, darn. She had to ask for that particular detail—and it was not a response I could fudge. Not after I spent all that time teaching her how to do a Google search a few years ago. "Birmingham," I muttered, hoping with everything in me that her hearing had suddenly decided to give up the ghost. But no, I was neither so lucky nor so blessed.

Her eyes lit up with delight as she clapped her hands. "Well, that's perfect. Birmingham is only a stone's throw from Millwood. You can at least come to the Sunday picnic. Those days usually aren't that busy at expos anyway, what with church and all."

I hesitated to tell her most of my clientele hadn't darkened a church door in years, if not ever in their lives, but I held my tongue. That might get her redirected on another tangent. She would be sure to then question my choice of careers—and the dissipating morals of the New South. Neither of which would be much preferred over the current topic.

I settled for the dutiful southern daughter response of, "Yes, Mama," and hoped the Almighty might somehow sideline John Mark, wherever it was he ended up.

♥ ♥ ♥

Late Sunday morning, I pulled my car into the packed parking lot of River Fork UMC, lips lifting in a reluctant smile. Decoration Day in North Alabama was more than cleaning up graveyards and replacing faded florals. It was a family reunion. And after coming nearly every Mother's Day since I was knee-high to a grasshopper, it was rather sad that this would be the last one. But with the minister retiring and his handful of sheep attending elsewhere, it wasn't surprising the little church was disbanding.

Cutting the engine, I scanned the graveyard and suddenly realized I was no longer a fan of the Almighty's sense of humor. John Mark stood two feet from the Townsend family headstone, deep in conversation with someone I vaguely recognized. Pasting on a bright smile, I wrapped all my southern manners around me like a cloak and lifted my box of store-bought cookies from the passenger seat.

The treats were a specialty assortment from a high-end pastry shop in Birmingham, but still not something from my own kitchen. So I bought them with the full understanding that I ran the huge risk of taking more than half of them home with me. I closed the driver's side door with my hip, then turned and did my best southern belle sashay across the newly trimmed lawn. My senses tingled a moment later. John Mark had spotted me.

Eat your heart out.

I'd chosen a sleeveless peach linen shift that fell just above the knee specifically to accent my creamy complexion and strawberry blonde hair. And judging by the head turns, it was the perfect "One That Got Away" dress. I shoved aside all the questions on why I would even care what he thought after he'd broken my heart so thoroughly.

"Wells, you made it!" Mama greeted me as if there was any doubt I would shirk her mandate.

Hands full of the cookie platter, I leaned in and touched my cheek to hers.

Mama held me to her and whispered, "Now, do be a dear and try not to make a scene. I wasn't really expecting John Mark to come, given all that happened between you two."

I pulled back and stared at her. Surely, she jested. If my presence was commanded, his certainly would have been too.

But as I read the real contrition in her eyes, I nodded and flashed a weak smile. Vowing to do my best, if only for her sake, I set the cookies at the end of the long buffet and made my way to the Fitzpatrick section of the graveyard.

Close and distant relatives were already camped out in lawn chairs trading family stories while they watched the younger generations play tag among the headstones. Grandma Willa's stone bore a tasteful wreath of silk magnolia leaves. My lips curved as memories of hugs drenched in magnolia-scented perfume wafted through me.

"Pretty tame compared to everyone else's headstone." John Mark's droll, thick accent rolled through me. I couldn't help my shiver. Ever since puberty deepened his childish tenor to a manly baritone, his voice called to something inside me. But the comment was an opening salvo that could not go unanswered.

"Grandma was more about understated elegance than tacky displays." I shot a pointed look to his own family's section covered in red, white, and blue silk carnations. Turning my gaze to him, my heart hiccupped as I nearly fell into his laughing cobalt eyes. *Drat this man. It's been five years. Lord, what is it about him that still ties me up in knots?*

John Mark searched my face as his teasing sobered to true admiration. "You look good, Wells."

Heat stole across my cheeks, but I forced myself to hold his gaze. He would not know how much he still affected me. Giving his wide shoulders, Kennedy haircut, and

Tommy Bahama ensemble my own thorough look, I said with reluctant honesty, "You do too."

"So what have you been up to? Still doing interior design in Atlanta?"

How do you know that's where I live? I flicked a quick glance back toward the buffet and found his mama and mine deep in conversation. *Of course.* Mama might have spared me the details all these years, but the southern family grapevine was alive and well.

My lips flattened into a thin line as I turned back to him. Raising my brows, I crossed my arms and studied him. "Is that really what you want to talk about, John Mark?"

He sighed, and his lips firmed into a rueful grimace. Shaking his head, he said, "No. It's not." He glanced at the rest of the gathering then toward a shaded area under the grove of mature oaks. "But can we talk in private? I'd rather not be the main topic of conversation."

My lips twitched. I flicked a quick glance around the gathering, counting the interested gazes that tried to look uninterested, and heaved a sigh. Even Great-Aunt Lydia, eyes clouded by cataracts, watched us with growing curiosity. *Batting a thousand.* I rolled my eyes. "Private or public, I believe we've already climbed to the top of everyone's list. But fine."

He offered his arm, and I slid my hand around his elbow, savoring the familiar chivalry. He laid his free hand over my fingers, and my pulse jumped just like it always had whenever we touched.

Dang it all, will my heart ever be free of this man? I swallowed the pang of misery as we walked into the cool surrounds of the drooping branches and thick, oak-leafed canopy.

I slipped my hand from his arm and clasped both in front of me, leveling an inquiring gaze on him. He'd requested the conversation, and I was for-dang-sure not going to start it.

John Mark tucked his hands in his pockets and rocked back on his heels, searching for words. I prayed they were ones I would want to hear.

"Wells, I know what I did was unforgivable, running off on you on our wedding day. But ... we were twenty-one. Just out of college."

He'd proposed at graduation as everyone in both of our families expected. The engagement was just long enough for Mama to plan a gorgeous bash and Daddy to slim down to fit into the tux he'd worn to their wedding. I had the dress of my dreams from *the* bridal shop in Birmingham. We were all set to live out our happily-ever-after. And then John Mark disappeared, leaving only a note saying, *I'm sorry. I love you, but I can't marry you.*

Pleading seeped into his gaze. He pulled his hands from his pockets and reached for me, then thought better of the action and dropped them to his sides. He took in a quick breath and shook his head. "You were the only girl I'd ever loved, and when I got to the church that day, I couldn't help but wonder if that was because I found the right person so early or because I had no experience with anyone else." He spread his hands wide. "And the thought of not knowing for sure scared the life out of me."

Lord, so far this is not the explanation I really wanted to hear. My hands clenched together into one fist as I squelched the sudden desire to wring John Mark's neck.

He glanced away, and when his eyes returned to mine, real sorrow lurked in their blue depths. "So I took the coward's way out, and I left. Moved to Nashville and got a job in the music industry. Once I was there, it was like a free-for-all. Parties. Festivals. Concerts. I went out, dated, and was even with one girl for nearly two years."

Two years? We were together almost all our lives.

Breath rushed between his lips on a resigned huff. "I knew she was expecting a proposal, but ... I just couldn't bring myself to do it. Every time I got close, all I could think about was you. And not that I left you so badly—"

My brows lifted as outrage crawled up my back, tensing my shoulders. *Buddy, you need to walk that one back fast if I'm going to keep my promise to Mama.*

John Mark gulped and had the good sense to pale, then managed to stammer a better explanation. "I mean, of course what I did was awful ... and I did think about that ... but what I meant was ..." He reached for my hand, slipping his fingers between mine and lacing them together.

Sweet memories poured through me, tugging me back to the first time we'd held hands under the tree near his house. We were thirteen, and after years of dreaming, he'd kissed me and promised to love me forever. Dang my heart, it had believed him.

John Mark took in a quick stabilizing breath as his gaze softened with remorse and hope.

My breath caught as I stared into his eyes. Wait. Wasn't that the same look he'd given me back then? Was it possible he did still love me? Fighting the tears filling my eyes, I prayed for him to say the words my heart so desperately wanted to hear.

"What I meant was, I knew leaving you on our wedding day was the biggest mistake I've ever made. I had found the woman I was supposed to spend my life with, and it was you."

Licking my lips, I swallowed the tears that clogged my throat. These were the words I wanted to hear, but could they really make up for the heartbreak and public humiliation?

"My company is transferring me to the Atlanta office next month." He glanced down at my naked ring finger then squeezed my hand. "Look, Wells, I know I was an idiot, but I still love you. And I also know I have no right to ask, but I'm going to ask anyway because I can't help myself. Can you forgive me? And can we start over?"

I swiped my free hand across my tear-dampened cheeks. "I would be a fool to give you the chance to break my heart a second time."

John Mark's lips parted as his eyes widened. Real worry lurked in their depths. He looked away, head bobbing in a slow, disappointed nod. "You have every right to walk away, Wells. And I deserve that. I know I do. But two wrongs only make another wrong. And we are right together. We have been for all our lives."

Oh, good Lord, if he's lying, I'm going to kill him. I took in a deep breath and let my heart overrule my head—just like it always did with him. That was how I ended up strapped to parachute jumping out of that perfectly good airplane after all. "I should walk away, John Mark. But here I am perfectly happy and ready to be a fool ... because ... I do love you." I shook my head in resigned certainty. "And heaven help me, I do not know why. So yes, I forgive you, and yes, we can start over."

His lips spread wide in a huge grin as he tugged me into his arms.

I slipped my hands up to cup his cheeks as my wounded heart swelled near to bursting. "Now kiss me, my adorable idiot, and let's make this a Decoration Day nobody will forget." As his lips met mine, delighted laughter, hoots, and hollers filtered through the trees. And I could almost hear all our ancestors joining their cheers.

JUNE

♥ ♥ ♥

ONE MIDSUMMER NIGHT

RENEE LEONARD KENNEDY

CADENCE HAD A TRUE-BLUE PROBLEM WITH FIRE ALARMS.

Using her personal rating scale, she would say it was a three-star difficulty. Yet her assistant reminded her of the Asheville incident involving a clothes steamer, a piercing alarm, and hotel evacuation.

As a wedding planner, neither mistakes—nor dating relationships—were acceptable. Then Cadence stumbled into a new four-star problem named Jay Cooper.

She caved. She melted all because *said* man held open the door for her at church. His Carolina blue polo emphasized his biceps, tanned and trained. His cheekbones rose when he smiled. His eyes transfixed her. The final straw was the buzzword most spoken of him: integrity. That sealed the deal. Cadence broke her steadfast golden rule held for the last ten years since her divorce. Ignore all men, except the client kind.

"Morning, Cadence." Jay Cooper spoke her name, not in need or frustration, but with care.

Sun blazed through the church door. Light thundered her peripheral vision. Her white sandals stalled on the foyer's floor. Cadence saw Jay in a new light.

"Are you okay?" he asked.

"I'm delicious." She blundered up the balcony stairs. She twisted to see him. "I'm deciduous." Her vocabulary and golden rule having failed her, she charged up the remaining stairs.

Later that evening, as she prepped to sear a steak, Cadence romanced the thought of a man in her life. As the sunset colored her world, the dog nosed her leg and whimpered. Her forgotten skillet scorched the coconut oil, surging smoke up to the farmhouse ceiling.

Five minutes later, she learned her romance's line of work. Captain Jay Cooper stepped over her door's threshold as the fire department rushed to inspect the house's interior. Gone was the friendly smile, the sunny warmth of the afternoon. For the second time in a day, he asked, "Are you okay?"

She did not feel delicious at this moment. Nor did Jay act as the man in church. Given his job, he was about one thing and one thing only: fire. And not the kind Cadence had been dreaming about minutes ago.

His walkie-talkie squawked. He pushed past Cadence and flipped the gas stove off. He set the offending cast iron aside.

"I'm sorry, Jay. The sunset. I watched it."

"You should never leave the kitchen with the stove on." Understandably, Jay Cooper had to condemn sloppy accidents. Saving lives and dwellings was his profession. Did his work mentality bleed into his personal life? She'd already spent years trying to be perfect for a man. Being considered less than and never enough wore the edges of her soul out.

"Will you forgive me, please?" She joined the fire crew heading to the door.

"Bad night," one of the men leaned in to tell her. "Cap's not slept."

She tapped her heart. "I truly appreciate the thorough check, Captain. Jay."

"Your batteries need changing." Nodding goodbye, he trudged the sidewalk to the fire truck. "Take care."

Cadence needed to be careful about swooning over this man. She hadn't had a crush since her ex-husband. Starting one now, at forty-one, seemed downright silly.

Her failures became episodic. One morning, Cadence heated coffee creamer on the gas stove rather than in the microwave. She retrieved a document from her office, making notes about the Beeker wedding, when the burn slithered from the kitchen to her nose.

She dashed to the stove, snapped the burner off, and tossed the blackened pot out the front door into her herb garden. Smoke rose to her ceiling. With the farmer's magazine, she swatted the offending air away from the fire alarm. Her dog hid underneath the couch. Cadence fanned faster.

Sure as sugar in tea, the blast blared, jarring her nervous system. She scooped up her phone and called the fire department, hoping to prevent their visit.

"Sorry, Cadence," the woman said. "You know, once triggered, the department has to come."

Thus she met Jay Cooper, barreling down her sidewalk.

"Oat milk. It burns faster than regular, I guess," she said.

"Cadence." His face was equal parts pity and annoyance. "Twice in two months? We talked about watching the stove." Jay cupped his chin.

"Let me make it up to the guys."

"Don't get distracted." He touched her arm. "Maybe get sticky notes to remind you."

Cadence heard him. This captain, all man sweat and buff build. If she leaned a few inches closer, her year would be decidedly scrumptious.

When she hit three alarms in three months, deserved shame overwhelmed her. The lodging logistics of the Beeker wedding were troubling. She burned the water out of the boiled eggs. Cadence had no idea eggshells could be blackened.

In her distraction, she was outright abusing the hard work and diligence of her local fire department. How ridiculous to think the charcuterie boards she'd sent the department could make up for her inexcusable actions.

Jay knuckled the granite countertop and gestured to her planner. "I've got Tuesday nights off."

Cadence gawked at Jay. The five-burner stove haunted her. "I need to do community service, don't I?"

He studied the farmhouse's low ceiling. "I'm going to teach you to cook. No distractions."

"Oh, good gravy." Cadence slumped and rested her head on the counter. "I'm a bad citizen."

Jay stepped back. "Thanks for inviting my men to fish the pond after the last call. But they're overworked." He pointed back to her planner. "Let's give them a break."

"Not touching the stove ever. I obviously have a problem." She slammed her planner shut. "Your time is as packed as mine."

"You need to eat."

"Takeout. They deliver. Just go about your life, Jay." He had no idea. She longed to be one of those cooks who managed multiple pots of rich flavors, to have the table set for guests—her own guests, not clients. To host a meal she'd specially prepared and they delighted in. To hear laughter and deep conversation fill these log walls instead of a whimpering dog, her Zoom calls, and an assistant asking her to sign checks.

Her behavior needed to end. "I'm covering the stove with granite so I'll not be tempted." Her dream of hospitality needed to die. The fire department was becoming exhausted. By her.

"Will you give me at least through June?" Jay Cooper loosened his chin strap. "Let's see where we get."

Maybe Jay could cure her bad habit in a month and some. Maybe she could learn to cook without distraction. At least his eyes, lip line, and mussed hair would be a joy to be near. She drew a solid line through the Tuesdays of April and May. "Wedding season is starting. But I'll make it work."

"Start tomorrow?" Jay lingered. "I'll bring supplies."

Her shoulders tensed. Somewhere between the dog's cry, the alarm's scream, and her heart's beat, Cadence crossed from crushing on the man to being his student. What would she wear?

As it turned out, her clothing selection did not matter. Her skirt and white shirt didn't hold up well with the smoke from the charcoal grill. After they pounded chicken between parchment paper, zucchini, watermelon, and meat sizzled on the grate.

"The one thing I wouldn't burn, watermelon. Now I'm grilling it."

"Wait until you taste it," he said.

Cadence had imagined enjoying dinners with dates and flirting over a meal. The thought caused a touch, if not a torrent, of fearful anticipation.

Yet this dream, too, was out of her reach.

"Sorry. Something came up." After serving her, Jay prayed over the meal, then cleaned the kitchen in a flash. His truck rumbled down the driveway, taillights signaling goodbye. She ate the unburnt dinner by herself. Since her company's motto was "dwelling on the bright side," Cadence rallied to this end.

She'd admired Jay's method and ability to teach. His slight smiles and hesitant laughs could be spun into a fantasy. The strength of his hands and forearms added points to the dream. Had something really come up? The burning arrows of this evening could have been one-sided. Cadence-sided. All about herbs, olive oils, and cooking times, Jay could as well have been Paula Deen—minus the butter and the muscles.

For the second lesson the following week, Jay brought her a combination indoor grill and panini maker. "Now, if you burn food, a smoke incident takes far longer with this machine." To add injury to insult, Jay held up a roll of caution tape. "Cadence, twenty-one days make a habit. Can we try something?"

"I'm game."

Jay zipped tape from her counters barricading her in the kitchen. If she wanted to leave, she had to stoop. "When you cook, stay in this zone. Reinforcement is key."

"I have client meetings at the table. A kitchen that looks like a crime scene isn't palatable."

"The visual will help to get you cooking safely here. A device-free zone."

"What if the client calls?"

"Wait thirty minutes?" Jay tucked the roll back into his bag and withdrew ingredients from the cooler. "Think of the return-on-investment. The alarm going off steals more of your time than cooking. Take calls only if appliances are off."

"Stove. Oven. Off." She straightened her jean shorts and t-shirt, having thought this outfit would be the perfect pairing with another grilled dinner. Jay showed no signs of noticing. "Yes, sir." Cadence threw in a salute for fun.

Shaking his head, Jay smiled. "That's 'captain' to you." He checked his cell, then set the device aside. "Grilled cheese can be dressed up in so many ways." He added spinach and four cheeses with avocado for interest. His phone sang an old Journey song.

"Now look who's distracted." The song, "Don't Stop Believing," would buzz in her head all night.

He ducked under the tape, a more perfect move never executed in the history of maledom.

"What about the rule? The panini maker is on."

He waved to shush her, then winked.

From crush to need to don't go, Cadence refrained from commenting on both his gestures because someone's life might be at stake. Jay clicked off the phone, and reentered the no-burn zone.

Funny how her exterior life paralleled her interior one. Something about her, she didn't know what, kept men at a distance. They looked, never moving past a glance. Easy conversation, certainly, but also as safe and heated as a LED candle. "Everything all right?"

"A private matter."

Her hope for one Jay Cooper evaporated. He was involved with someone.

Cadence feigned confidence. "You broke the rule. Can't leave the barrier with appliances on."

"Yes, but I trusted you to prevent any fires." Clearly, Mr. Cooper was here only to teach the spinster to cook and not burn. Nothing more, nothing less. Jay lifted the panini lid, and steam slipped out. The unalarming kind. He breathed, and his shoulders relaxed.

"I would like to have the department over," she said.

He shook his head. "That's a lot of extra work for you."

"I host weddings twenty times a year. I got this down. It'll be easy."

Hoping he'd stay, Cadence pulled out two of her Italian

ceramic plates. "I'll cut the cantaloupe. Got it down the road." She reached over the barricade tape to get the cutting board.

As they carried their plates to the side porch, Cadence smiled. Her pond captured the sunset. A breeze danced. The first summer fireflies sparked.

"Tell me one thing about yourself." She sipped a Red Rock ginger ale. The taste bit her tongue.

"Not much that's interesting."

Cadence picked up a quarter of her panini. No way would she break the silence. If he wasn't the type to talk about his life, she and he would stare into the sunset. Quietly.

Jay swallowed the ginger ale, followed by a coughing fit. She touched her napkin to her lips. His eyes watered. He cleared his voice. A deer blew a warning to its young near the hay field. A hummingbird reverberated in the air.

"You don't give up easily." He sipped more carefully this time.

"Friendships are often built on awkward silences." A friend's son had said that about dating. But Jay didn't have to know that. If he wouldn't talk—and she would almost bet on it—then she would feast on the memories he'd given her thus far. Since it seemed a poetic night, Cadence had an urge to toss white roses onto pond water and sink in the silt.

"Tell me about the Beeker wedding."

Cadence breathed from her stomach up. She could talk about this. "A couple is renting out the house and using the side yard for their vows and reception. A family of acquisition lawyers. This could reach national publication."

"Fancy," Jay said.

"Not so much fancy. But the theme is. One Midsummer Night. The bride loved the pitch. The longest day of the year spent with the one you'll love forever."

Jay leaned back. "This is special to you."

The birds dipped their wings in the pond. "It's more than special. It's the joy of sharing this land and the dream with others."

Stretching his arms on the teak bench, he focused on her eyes. "This evening's been perfect."

On the third lesson, Jay had taken her hand and prayed over the lemon chicken. "Amen," they said together. He held her hand for seconds longer, then let go. "About relationships."

She swallowed and wanted to snatch his hand back.

"How many years since your divorce?" he asked.

"You first."

Jay pulled his napkin out of its knot—all the brides, thanks to social media, were into knotted napkins. "It's been five years. She divorced me and eloped in Vegas." Jay shrugged. "My daughter, Tonya. She's eighteen. The one who calls on the phone." He placed the napkin in his lap. "She lives with her mom. How about you, Cadence?"

She breathed deeply. "It's been over ten years."

"Nothing's worked out?"

Without having to look, she re-knotted her napkin. The sun slipped behind the walnut and cherry trees, glowing the golden hour. "Not enough time with work." Her lie slipped low like the sun.

After the fourth dinner, Jay took Cadence's hand while they strolled across the field.

"What was your wedding like?" Jay asked.

Did she have to mention the Vegas hotel? "It was a small affair." A rental preacher and slot machines. The reception was the buffet. The honeymoon suite needed an exterminator.

"If you could do it over again, it'd be the Midsummer idea?"

"Yes, in the likelihood that ever happens." She was

throwing her perfect wedding for someone else. At least Priscilla Beeker was worth it. Cadence thumped the walking stick she carried ever since copperhead skins had been found.

"You come off as the independent sort. But you're a romantic."

That was true. However, commitment would wear the pants in her next marriage, if that ever happened. "I've seen so many relationships built solely on this." She waved a hand up and down her torso.

Jay cleared his throat. "Men notice that. Certainly."

"Do guys ever look at a woman's character?" she asked.

"They'd be fools not to."

Jay unhitched the gate then held the metal door open for her.

She passed by him, brushing his shoulder. "Maybe some women are meant to go it alone."

"Not you, Cadence." Jay pivoted in front of her. "You have to know that."

"It's not been very promising."

He wiped his hands across his face.

She wished he'd say something, but the night ended beside his truck, the peacock down the way calling, and the dog whining for him. Jay reached up and squeezed her shoulder. As the friendly type, he could string her along for years. Cadence had no desire to be somebody's indefinite line.

Lesson five with the hot wok ended with promise. Jay tucked his arm around her shoulder as they strolled to his truck. She paused. "Look behind you."

They turned in harmony. The moon shone over her farmhouse.

"It was a good night," he said.

"Yes, it was, Captain."

As he drove away, her cell buzzed. They had talked until the moon had crossed the sky.

The next lesson—following a dinner of fried apples and eggs with salmon—Cadence hugged Jay. Or Jay collided with Cadence. One or the other. Holding each other, they sighed, then laughed at the mirrored response.

Cadence wanted to give in to this moment. But the what-ifs snapped that desire away. "What are we doing, Jay?"

His head bent to her ear. "Goodnighting."

She wanted to say stop. But her heart said otherwise. He pressed her head to his shoulder.

The spring temperature had dropped by lesson seven. Jay arranged logs in the firepit to foil cook vegetables and chicken. They shared a blanket together with their feet perched on the warm stones. Tuesday had become her favorite day of the week.

Class number eight began an hour early with the fire engine's arrival. Cadence had wanted to prove she had overcome her problem. The Jefferson bride was overdue a decision though. She'd stepped out of the no-burn zone to grab her phone from the office. It had taken four minutes for the fire alarm to sound, and four minutes to remember she forgot to call her electrician about changing the smoke alarm to a heat sensor.

The truck wailing from the crossroad, Cadence rushed down the long driveway. "It's all right," she shouted at Jay over the horns. Cadence was mortified. "I've been so careful." Jay leaped out of the truck. "The garlic cooked so fast."

"Another bridal panic, Cadence?" He brushed past her.

She grabbed his arm as a few firemen passed by.

"Cadence, I'm on duty now."

"I wanted to surprise you."

His lips pressed tight, Jay hovered over the

smoking skillet she'd plopped in the sink. "You did that. Had flames, I see."

She grasped at his hand. "Shrimp scampi."

"The Jefferson wedding?" Jay shook her off.

She thumped her fist against her chest. "I don't know what's wrong. Before I started this business, I never set off alarms. And yes, the bride wants to change the setup. With a week to go."

He picked up the skillet. "You ruined a world-class pan."

"I'm glad I hadn't added the shrimp yet."

"It could have been so much worse." Jay turned the faucet to hot water. "Class is over."

The skillet sizzled underneath the flow. "Stay for a panini, Jay?" She hated the desperation in her voice. Yet it was the most authentic emotion in her at this moment.

"I have a report to fill out. I can't anymore, Cadence. Lord knows, I worry all the time about when you're going to burn this place down." Jay gestured between them. "I can't. This."

"I'll swear off the stove. I promise. Only do take-out and salads."

"No more lessons. No more dinners." Jay dropped the skillet back in the sink with a clang. "I'm going to ask for a transfer. Asheville has some openings."

"Because of me?"

"I can't lose anyone else." Jay left and wandered up the sidewalk.

Cadence imagined running after him and hauling herself into the fire truck, begging him for one more chance. Jay Cooper had been the bright star of her weeks, the balance she needed after watching other women walk down the aisle. Now she knew the truth. Where this smoke was, there was fear, on both sides.

The fire truck headed back to the station. Cadence fingered the drooping tape. She should have stayed in the no-burn zone, no matter what. Her conscience and heart would have been far safer.

To say goodbye to the department, Cadence dropped off several large boxes of Bill's chicken wings. Personal responsibility nagged at her soul. She got honest about the last months and wrote Jay a note asking for forgiveness. As the weddings stacked up, Cadence ignored the loss. The sunsets at the farm settled her soul. A smidgen.

The pinnacle of her season, the Beeker wedding, came at last. Thousands of twinkle lights, pedestals of tropical plants, and gossamer fabrics decorated her yard. Bright LED balls floated in the pond.

Days from the rehearsal dinner, the parents and fiancé had landed an acquisition of a lifetime with the deadline due over the weekend. The wedding was canceled, with Cadence and the vendors paid in full. The bride relocated to an Italian destination and, of course, was pleased. "Celebrate Midsummer Night on the farm for us," the mother of the bride said. "We'll handle Tuscany."

Some women.

Yet, here she was, blessed with vendors from food to pyrotechnics. She danced at the thought of sharing this, but had to hype herself up for a phone call. "The Beeker wedding fell through," Cadence said to Jay's voicemail. She cleared her voice. "The party is all set up. Tell the off-duty guys to bring their wives and girlfriends."

Alone or with others, Cadence was determined to spend this longest day of the year outside. Adjusting a straying rose on the pergola, she hoped carloads of people would come through. She trod the yard barefoot in her new, flowy dress.

Cadence flipped on the master switch, and lights shimmered across an acre. The sound system played a waltz. She poured local sparkling muscadine juice into a tall-throated glass. Car lights reflected off the crystal.

Cadence smiled, a foreign action of late. Jay and she might never again cook, share dinner, or gaze at the moonlight together, but he wouldn't let his men miss out on this. Doors slammed. Women's voices raised, and the men's echoed the same excitement. She removed the silver lids from the food.

"Eat, drink, and be merry," she yelled to the men and their beloveds. "Fireworks at ten." Cadence wove around the new boxwood maze. Delight and despair accompanied her. She fiddled with the knob of the telescope, the groom's contribution, to see the stars.

"I thought you'd be with the pyro guys."

Startling at his voice, Cadence knocked her eye against the lens. "Ouch. Jay."

He studied her eyebrow. "Might get tender there."

Cadence lifted her chin to meet his eyes. She shouldn't have. Seeing their brilliance reminded her how hard she'd worked to forget about him. "Thanks for telling the men."

He moved closer.

Cadence reared backwards and picked a path through the maze. "You quit me because I made a mistake. Huge, I know, a false alarm." Her dress swished with the unexpected summer breeze. "You left."

He grabbed her hand. "The last months haven't been the same."

Cadence jerked her hand away. "Missed the barricade tape, no doubt." Cadence hurried down the maze, running her fingertips along the boxwood. "Don't use me just because you're lonely."

"You scared me."

She paused, her bare feet wiggling against the sandy path.

"Cadence, please."

Her toes clinched the ground.

"I want more for us," he said.

The bubbling of the nearby fountain soothed her hurt places. Jay had shown up. Cadence could open up too.

A breeze scattered weeping cherry blossoms. She held her palm out and caught the petals, nature calling them to play. "So, Mr. Cooper, you have to do one thing."

"Excuse me?"

"Take your shoes off." Cadence brushed her hands through the water falling from the top tier of the fountain, then meandered down the lane. "Or you have to leave, Captain."

A hiking shoe sailed beside her. Then another. His feet rustled through the grass. She twirled.

Eyes intense, Jay Cooper bolted to Cadence. "This is crazy, coming from someone my age."

"I'm not interested in just living with you." She turned her back on him. Jay snagged the bow to her dress.

"Me neither, Cadence." Jay pulled the bow to slowly spin her around. "Spend the longest day of the year with me?"

Shivering, she crossed her arms. "Then what?"

"A lifetime, Cadence." Jay wrapped his arms around her.

She tilted her head skyward. Perhaps this night would be magical after all.

"A small event, Cadence. The barefoot thing. Definitely."

Her hands slipped up his back. "Can we have fireworks too?"

"Only if you light them." Underneath the Midsummer sky, with Venus burning bright, Jay kissed Cadence. In concert with the katydids, their hearts rang the good alarm for this timeless night.

JULY

SPARKS

ROSE HATHAWAY

"I'M GOING TO BE REALLY HONEST. I AM PROBABLY THE least-deserving person to be here." Gabe said this, flicked off his noise-canceling headphones, and tossed a sheepish look at the woman behind the fold-up check-in desk.

She sported a red bandana on her head and a tank top jean jacket. Cicadas screamed from the trees as the soupy Midwest humidity caused Gabe's hair to stick up on all ends.

No amount of gel could tame the do.

"Sorry, dear." The woman flashed a smile at him and then her badge. Stars speckled the "Marie" on her tag. "Could you repeat that?"

"I." By instinct, he reached for the headphones. A woman nearby sucked on a plastic water bottle, causing the casing to crunch too loudly. Instead, Gabe clasped his elbow. "I feel like I don't deserve to be here. I know you guys have limited spots."

Marie squinted at him. Then she flicked away a bee that buzzed too close. Gabe's ears filled with ringing from the noisy insect.

"You're Gabe, right?" She slashed a yellow highlight across his name on the paper before her. "Why do you say that you shouldn't be here?"

"Well, I'm not a soldier or vet—"

He motioned to a man with a buzz cut wearing an Army t-shirt. A woman with platinum blonde hair hung onto his shoulder with her arm.

"—and I'm not someone who owns a dog or pet that gets scared because of fireworks."

Whines from a German Shepherd nearby pierced his eardrums.

"—so therefore, I feel like I'm taking up space."

To occupy his thoughts away from the noises, he scanned the brochure they'd handed him when he pulled into the parking lot. A man in the picture, wearing Boy Scout-like gear, smiled at the photographer snapping the photo. Beside him, a big block of white text against a navy-blue background read:

> *Welcome to Camp Taciturn. Although this is usually a spot for Scouting troops to camp out throughout the year, we have blocked it off for the Fourth of July weekend.*
>
> *Started by couple Marie and Ted Lentium, Marie noticed that although America is enthusiastic during Fourth of July celebrations, it can often forget the needs of the very same people who fought for its freedom; how they may be recovering from the battlefield and don't do well in loud, noisy environments.*

"I noticed how Ted would get really nervous during fireworks. So we found a campground far enough away from the noise," Marie said, upon the inaugural year of Camp Taciturn's Fourth of July weekend program. "And of course, we couldn't keep it to ourselves. So we invited everyone in."

Those wanting to get away from the Fourth of July fireworks are welcome to this quiet weekend in the woods.

"Although Ted has since passed," Marie says, "I know that he's blessing this holiday away from the noise."

Gabe glanced up from the brochure.

Was this the same Marie—?

Marie wicked sweat off her upper lip and reached for a can of bug spray. Fumes from the aluminum can reached Gabe's nose.

"Gabe, you're the one with the high sensitivity to noise, right?"

Mouth dry, he nodded. Well, high sensitivity to every sense, if he were being perfectly honest. Light burned his eyes if he ambled into a wash of sunlight unwarned. Almost always, he wore a pair of sunglasses to take the edge off.

He didn't really like touch from most human beings either, because he could feel each prickle, each pinch, in a deeper sense than most people. And as far as noise went ...

The noise-canceling headphones traveled with him everywhere.

"Then you are more than welcome here," she said at a near-whisper, as though understanding. This had to be the Marie mentioned in the brochure. Someone married to a husband with a sensitivity to noise would get someone like Gabe.

As she handed him a name tag, he forced himself not to

look at her. To take in those beautiful brown eyes or that deep, tan skin.

Because if he knew anything about his condition ... it would form a burden for any significant other. He tried and failed in his college years to procure dates. But they shied away when they learned how many accommodations the college campus made for him.

Once, a girl who tolerated a few coffee dates said to him, "Seriously? You have a *single* room on the top floor—?"

Top floor because any of the lower levels would endure the footsteps pounding from above. That could keep him up all hours of the night.

"—and go into a fetal position when someone's bass music gets too loud? Honestly, Gabe, man up. It can't be that bad."

His college in particular forced all freshmen to endure dorm life for their first year at the university. But sophomore year, he moved off campus.

He clipped the name tag onto his shorts pocket. He made sure to put on the knee-length capris, because if he wore the pants too short, then the name tag would brush against his legs. And that would bug him for the rest of the day.

Already he had to limit his closet to certain fabrics. Otherwise, ants would crawl all over his skin until he yanked the outfit off.

Marie beamed at him and pointed at a list. "All of our activities today are great for people with sensory issues. I'm about to hand over my shift to another worker, so let me know if you want me to join you for anything."

Something about the sparkle in her smile set a different kind of fireworks exploding in his stomach.

Does she really want to hang out with me? Because she pitied him? The tone of her voice didn't indicate that. Maybe she truly wanted to get to know him.

He avoided eye contact and perused the list.

- Trampoline jumping
- Yoga
- Painting and mocktails

His eyes stopped on the third one down. Marie appeared to follow the trail of his index finger that went down each item on the itinerary.

"We have a lot of recovering alcoholics here, so we want to be conscientious about what we serve." She leaned in, hand cupped against her mouth. "But you'll swear our virgin watermelon sangria is the real thing."

He smiled at this.

Gabe hated the taste of alcohol. How it burned on the way down his throat until he choked and coughed. It took him ages to find a group of friends that would hang with him in his mid-twenties, since most of his peers wanted to occupy bars after work.

"Would you—?" He glanced over his shoulder at a circular trampoline, situated over a lake. "Wanna go there?"

She nodded.

"First, let's get some life vests on. And honey, you can wear those headphones if you want. I see your how your fingers keep itching for them. Remember." She reached a hand out, probably to touch his shoulder, then thought better of it and clasped her fingers together. "This is your vacation. Your getaway. We don't judge here."

Light exploded in his chest again.

He slipped on the headphones, and the sounds around him muffled. Once they reached the life jacket shed, an algae stench punched him in the nostrils. Still, for time with Marie, he grinned-and-bore clasping the damp buckles on his life jacket.

Then they set off onto the trampoline.

They each took turns, bouncing each other as high as

they could go. Others swarmed the trampoline. At first, Marie wouldn't let them on. She eyed Gabe for permission. He massaged a rug burn on his calf and nodded.

People bounced along with them, sending him soaring into the air during his turn to get "bounced."

His own laughter rang in his ears. At one point, the noise-canceling headphones slid off and almost into the water. But he hardly heard the noise. Whatever drifted into his ears sounded like peace.

Like a song he'd yearned his whole life to hear.

After yoga and a snack at the canteen—both of them opted for noiseless foods such as gummy worms—they met in a wood, air-conditioned building to paint.

A woman with a soothing voice instructed them on how to paint sparklers onto a canvas. Gabe stroked pink against a "sparkler stick" on the painting as Marie suckled from a straw. Ice clinked in her drink as she set it down on the table.

Her elbow perched on her chair as she leaned back and admired Gabe's painting.

"You're really good at that."

Embers glowed in his intestines. "Thanks. I think it's the environment. I could live here forever."

With you.

He didn't add that part, but he wanted to. Even in the short few hours together—with so few words exchanged—she made him feel like a firework. Effervescent, trailing lights against the backdrop of an inky sky.

Marie sighed. "Me too. Really missed it. I didn't go last year. It was too hard with Ted passing just a few months before, you know?"

She drew her knees up to her chest and fetal-positioned herself on the classroom chair.

He dipped his brush into water. Pink mixed with a swirl of white.

Then he reached for his drink. He'd asked for a mocktail mojito.

Mint tanged the back of his throat as he sipped, and sugar crystals coated his tongue.

He set the glass down on the table and placed his headphones onto the crook of his neck. Her voice had come out muffled before, but he still caught the words.

"I'm sorry, Marie. That must've been hard."

She nodded. A single finger reached up to swipe away moisture from her waterline.

"It was. He was this guy who noticed everything. Who would hear noise in the quiet and see emotions in a stony face. And when he was gone, it—"

Another sigh. She pinched her straw and swirled it in the glass. Ice cubes whirled around in an endless twister.

"—it was like all the detail had gone from my life. Days blurred into one another. Like one firework after the other, noisy and numb. I kept forgetting to make myself food. He was always so thoughtful with the little things. So I decided that no matter what, I'd force myself to come here this year."

Gabe plucked his brush out of the water and daubed it on a paper towel. Light pink bled into the white.

"Why did you come?"

"Because it's quiet here, Gabe. And when you force yourself to be in the quiet, you start to hear beautiful things. See beautiful things." A twinkle caught in her eye as she looked at him. "It's like when one wonderful song ends, and you wait for the next one to start."

Silence wrapped them in a hug as they caught glimpses of one another.

He set his brush down and placed his hand onto hers.

"When do you think the next song is starting, Marie?"

Her lips curved up her cheeks. "Right about now, I would say."

AUGUST

ALL'S FAIR

ROSE HATHAWAY

CHEATING IS NEVER OKAY. UNLESS YOU RUN A CARNIVAL game at a Minnesota Fair booth.

A man in an American flag-design tank top with sweat stains on the pits holds back a grimace after his last ring toss. The plastic blue ring clinks against the glass bottle and ricochets to the side, toward the booth next to mine housing some game with rubber ducks in a lazy river and magnets.

I perch a hand on my hip and beam my best smile at him. Thank goodness the sun has decided to obscure most of my view. He looks murderous.

"Better luck next time!"

He mutters something under his breath. Music from the nearby Ferris wheel muffles his words. Probably for the best.

Doesn't he know by now that carnival games are

purposely rigged against the players? A few paces away, a person hosts a pop-a-balloon-with-a-dart booth. During a break yesterday, he told me how he rigs customers out of their money—deflated balloons, dull darts.

As for my booth, well, those rings don't fit too well around the necks of those bottles. To win, you have to flick your wrist just right.

The line for my game has, at last, dwindled—three hours into my shift. I swipe the sheen of sweat on my forehead off with the back of my hand and nod once to my assistant, Aisha. She tucks her sunglasses into her frizzy hair and fans herself with her polo shirt.

"Wanna go on break, Ju?"

I lick my lips and discover they've grown parched. A family with large stuffed animals tucked under their arms—likely won from a more *fair* fair game—passes by our booth. The sun scorches the pathways that loop around the various rides and stalls, until the once muddy roads now cake shoes in dry dirt.

I squat behind the rows of bottles to find my Hydro Flask. Unscrewing the top, I wince at how empty the vessel feels. Probably need to refill it soon.

Despite the cheery carnival music in the background and the rev of a chainsaw from a wood carving show happening a few stalls down, I can hear the distinct growl of my stomach. Why did I ignore breakfast this morning?

"Empty?" Aisha bobs her chin at my water bottle.

I tip my head back and gulp one last swig of warm water. "Now it is." I gasp, lips still crackled.

"Ju, you've been going nonstop. Why dontcha you stop there at that booth," she gestures at one with yellow block letters advertising various drinks, "get lemonade, and bring a girl back some funnel cake, eh?"

Funnel cake. The ghosts of powdered sugar dance on my tongue. That does sound nice.

"Fine. I'll get us each a plate. But you better pay up the five dollars you owe me for the funnel cake the *minute* I get back to the booth."

She snorts and attempts to wave over a couple with bags of cotton candy bundled in their fists. She fails to draw their attention. "Girl, I couldn't cheat you out of two cents. You've got an elephant's memory."

Oooh, elephant ears. Wouldn't say no to those.

And yes, she's right. After my fair share of cheaters, I make sure that no one cuts corners around me.

I flick an auburn braid off my shoulder. Should've put the hair up into a full bun today. I can feel the sweat on the back of my neck as the hair sticks to the skin. Goodness, what a sunburn I'll carry home with me today.

"You're right." I weave my way around the rows of bottles and head toward the booth. "I don't take kindly to cheaters. So you best get that five dollars?"

She rolls her eyes and reaches for her purse.

I whirl around and dodge some Army men asking if anyone wants to stop by their booth for a free t-shirt. A winding line trails from the lemonade booth. I glimpse the menu and try not to gawk at the prices.

For someone who's worked several days at a fair, you'd think I would've gotten used to a pulled pork sandwich going for $9. Then again, I can't talk. We charge $5 for three tosses at our station.

When I near the front of the queue, the scent of sizzling meat coming from inside the mobile food station makes my temples pound. Yeesh, I may order enough food to make my bank account weep.

As I approach the front of the line, a pimpled teenager leaves his station as "order taker" and bounds out of the back of the vehicle. He races toward a whirling ride.

Can't blame him. Even though none of us dwell under

the luxury of AC here, these food vehicles pack a lot of heat, thanks to fryers and heated food.

Another figure supplants the teenage boy from his station. A man with a decent tan, well-trimmed beard, and dark eyes. Shoot. I know him.

"What can I get for—" He pauses, grin cutting up his cheek. And he has the audacity to brighten, happy to see me. "Ju, is that you? I thought I spotted you in that booth earlier, but I've been working all morning."

"Wow. So this fair is just full of cheaters, isn't it?"

His shoulders droop.

Oh yes, Jackson, don't think I've forgotten about when we dated. When I found you buddying up with your ex in a bar. Touching her shoulder, laughing, seemingly forgetting that we were supposed to rendezvous there and head to a local restaurant for a date.

Didn't help that after I left the bar in a hurry, his ex texted me.

> **Jackson's Ex:** Sorry that Jack didn't have the guts to tell you. But maybe it's better this way. So you two can break off more easily.

And break off we did. Two angry texts and two pints of ice cream later, I'd written him out of my life, until today ...

Sweat stings my eyeballs. Goodness, we've had quite a hot August today, haven't we?

"Listen, Ju, you never allowed me to explain myself about that."

I hold up a palm and wrinkle my nostrils at the scents coming from a nearby 4-H barn. "Now's not the time. I'm on break and—" I glance over my shoulder at Aisha. No one has swung by our booth— "and my assistant probably needs some relief and—"

"Her? She's stopped by here about five times. She's fine."

Had Aisha taken that many breaks? And goodness, girl, how many lemonades do you need to order?

I blink away the images that conjure into my head of discarded cups with lemon designs imprinted on them. For some reason, I'd assumed some fair attendees had discarded those in our game tent.

"Listen." I wipe the perspiration from my eyes and, despite myself, tuck some strands of greasy hair behind my ears. Even after everything, I still want to look nice around him. I curse and thank myself for wearing waterproof eyeliner today. "I just came here to order some lemonade and funnel cake. I really do need to get back soon."

Wasps buzz around the lemonade cups. Maybe I should go for water instead.

I arch my back, and my heart deflates at the size of the lines that snake through the other food booths. If I ditch my spot now, I won't get food for well over twenty minutes. My stomach, the drama queen she is, growls.

"Tell you what." He slaps his palm against the metal counter. "I win the game at your booth, and if I do, you owe me one ride on the Ferris wheel to explain what really happened." He holds up his phone. "Since you blocked my number before I could."

Ugh, seriously?

A headache threatens to roll into my temples like a thundercloud. I can't go much longer without food. "Fine, but when you lose, you immediately make my assistant and I funnel cakes for free." I notch an eyebrow. "And you hightail it out of the fair and never speak to me again."

He folds his arms. "Well, that doesn't seem fair."

"Neither does being in a two-year relationship and dropping it all for an ex—who told you you couldn't tip waitresses because she was jealous and thought they were hitting on you. Pretty upstanding woman, huh?"

Jackson deflates, firms his jaw, holds out a hand. "Fine. Deal."

He pops his head back into the shade of the vehicle to ask someone to take his place, and we both march toward my game booth. Aisha detangles the sunglasses out of her hair and quirks one side of her lip.

"This looks like trouble. Where's the funnel cake, sis?"

"Give this *fine* gentleman three rings." I cross my arms. "This'll be good."

She holds up five dollars she must've pinched between two fingers for a solid ten minutes when I stood in line. Have to hand it to her, at least she has no intentions of cheating on me.

"Keep it." I gesture at her purse and re-fold my arms. "We're going to get some free fried food in a moment."

Aisha rehomes her five dollars and drops three rings into Jackson's palms.

I release my arms and feel the empty space on my ring finger. A sigh nests in my gut. He'd talked about proposing, three months back, before the day at the bar. "Your move, Jackson." I clear my throat. Goodness, I hadn't realized something had gotten stuck in my windpipe. I choke whatever it is down.

He flicks the first one. It bounces off a bottle in the middle.

"Two tries left." I stop pinching my ring finger.

Jackson's usual bright demeanor has darkened. Maybe he thought this game would go far more in his favor. If he sat in a food stall straight across the pathway from me, maybe he'd had plenty of chances to observe the differences in the throws. Which winners actually lassoed a ring around a bottle's neck.

He tosses again. This time a ring spindles around a

bottle toward the front before flying off. It lands near a woman who holds a large tub of fries in her hands.

"One more chance." I glance at the stuffed animals that hang from the ceiling instead of at him.

Gosh, the sweat is really pouring into my eyes. I blink it away ... wait, no it's trailing down my cheeks. Tears?

I swipe at the moisture with my fingertips. Hadn't I gotten over him? Why does he still make my stomach flutter?

He holds up a ring and peers at me through the hole, staring deep into my soul. Then he shuts his eyes and folds the plastic object into his fingers. Exhales. Regrips the ring. He flicks his wrist, and the ring soars toward the back of the rows of bottles.

I watch it slam onto the neck of a green bottle. It doesn't blast off. The ring stays. He won the bet.

Saltiness fills my tongue as I lick my upper lip. "Well, I guess you—"

Jackson holds up one finger and darts off to the food van. Minutes later, he emerges with two funnel cakes and a large cup of lemonade. "One for each of you. I know you're hungry." A plate slides into my palms. Powdered sugar flurries onto my shoes. "Once you've eaten, meet me at the Ferris wheel?"

Before I have a chance to respond, he zooms back into his food stall and helps the next customer.

One full stomach later, I meet him in a winding queue and pull out a twenty. He shields the money with his palm, shakes his head. "On the house. Listen." He palms his neck. "About that day—"

I redirect the twenty to the ticket boy. He makes change and hands me a stack of bills and two tokens for the ride.

"Yes?" I brush my finger against my lips to make sure I've gotten rid of all the powdered sugar.

"She asked me to come to the bar to give me an

engagement gift. I'd planned to propose that night and—I didn't think anything of it. She hangs there a lot, so I figured it was a good meeting point. Hence why I texted you to meet me there, and I'd drive us both to the restaurant after."

He sighs as we sidle into the bench on the next available Ferris wheel car. A worker barricades us in.

"The shoulder touch, the laughter, whatever you saw ... it wasn't anything. Only later did I find out that she'd set up the whole thing to make you jealous. So you'd walk out and she could pretend like we'd gotten together."

I brush my fingertips against my jean shorts.

Part of me wants to believe it. "She did ... she did get jealous of wait staff, thinking they were hitting on you. I guess it isn't out of character."

The ride kicks off with a groan, and we sail toward the clouds in silence.

"So." He grips the metallic part of the car like it's an arm rest. "I know we can't start from where we were. But is there a way to start over?"

Butterflies attack my stomach. I can't look at him because I already feel the tears prick my eyes. Two pints of ice cream didn't get rid of him.

I chew on my lip and release a sigh. "You know what, Jackson. I think we can more than start over. How about a date, after we close up shop, to talk more things over?"

He perks up, brightness filling his face. "Really?"

"Yeah." I smile and allow my shoulders to relax. "I think it's more than fair."

SEPTEMBER

♥ ♥ ♥

TAKE YOUR PICK

ROSE HATHAWAY

ON A SCALE OF GOLDEN DELICIOUS TO HONEYCRISP, I'LL rate Tony Smith a Red Delicious. Bland, tasteless—and it could be this toasty September sun shining down on us—but he does also appear a bit waxy.

I feign a smile at my best friend Johnny as he stands next to the date I've picked out for him, Rose.

Johnny and I agreed that at thirty years old, and with most of the people in our church's young adult group having paired off with someone by the age of twenty-five, we needed to "help a brother/sister out."

So we decided to go on a group date. And pick out the date for our bestie.

From what I can tell from Rose, I hope I've secured a perfect match. She wears a sunflower yellow dress and talks in her loudest stage voice. As a shy introvert, he enjoys listening to conversations and for someone to take the lead.

As for me, Johnny set me up with ... Tony.

And from our car ride over here, our conversations mostly consisting of me trying to force Tony to talk about the weather—I can tell this apple-picking date will go on for some time.

See, I can do silence with Johnny. Because quiet between us is more like an understanding. That we don't always have to talk all the time. That in those special moments, we can stare out the windows on the highway and watch the verdant Ohio tree leaves fade into all the autumn colors.

But with Tony. The quiet feels like a rock in my gut. Unnatural, off.

Johnny's eyes dart to mine. He mimics my expression before turning back to Rose, who is in the middle of talking about her favorite types of apples.

She swings her apple-picking basket in one hand, insisting that they, *"Have to* get Granny Smith."

I stare down the rows of pinkish apples before me with a wooden picket sign next to the trees declaring the type of apple, "Gala."

"So, Tony." I grip the basket in my hands and try to pipe my voice as high as Rose's. My other hand, sweaty, grapples with the skirt on my blue gingham dress.

Johnny has affectionately called it my "Dorothy outfit." I smile at the thought. My lips falter when I meet Tony's burning gaze again.

"Umm, should we go with Johnny and Rose? Stick together and find the best apples?"

He shakes his head. "We should split off."

Wow, I got four words out of him at one time. Better than the one-word responses I got in the car.

"Oh, okay." The rock grows larger in my stomach again.

Much as I love one-on-one time with people like Johnny, I tend to prefer bigger groups.

Because in a crowd of people, one is bound to have deeper conversations.

"Which type of apples do you want?"

He shrugs.

After several seconds of painful silence, I gesture at the Gala apple row. "This seems like a crowd pleaser." I wave to Johnny and Rose. "Meet you both at the food stalls in half an hour?"

Releasing my skirt, I point at the food vendors in the parking lot. On the way in, the thoughts of Mexican street corn and sizzling burgers stirred up my hunger. Thankfully, the workers here also have no problems with us sampling the apples.

As long as we paid the twenty-dollar fee for the basket.

It seems that other patrons had no problems with giving these fruits a try. Apples with bites taken out of them litter the grass. Bees poke out of every corner and crevice of the ground.

"So, Tony." I've started just about every conversation like this today. "You mentioned in the car that you work in mechanical engineering. That's really cool." I pluck a juicy pink fruit—with green streaks going down the sides—off of a higher stem. Even though apple-picking season started only a month ago, most Ohioans have grazed through the lower branches of these rows of trees. "Tell me more about that."

Tell me more about that.

During my years of college journalism, our professors insisted that that question could draw even the shyest of turtles out of their shells.

In fact, back when I met Johnny in our early twenties at the young adult group, I found him huddled in the basement of our small group leader in a beanbag chair.

Two men slammed a ping-pong back and forth nearby him, drowning out most of the conversations that surrounded us.

"So, Johnny," I'd said to him, balancing a plate of veggies and dip in my palms. "You, earlier, had said that you don't want any kids. Which is a pretty rare find with most guys in the church. Tell me more about that."

Thus sparked a three-hour long conversation between the two of us that night.

And we'd never stopped talking since.

Tony lifts and drops his shoulders. His thick fingers play with a leaf on a lower branch.

"There's not much to tell. I don't really like my job much."

Well, I suppose two sentences is no small triumph. I plop the apple in our basket as we sally down the rows. Children shriek and skirt past us, dodging a wasp they must've angered.

I breathe through my nostrils, long and slow. I gotta crack this guy somehow. Surely some sort of conversation can get going.

"Oh?" After we've filled our basket with four Galas, I motion for us to step through the trees toward the Fuji trees. "Are you looking for another place to work?"

"No."

Dang it, Elise, you just committed a journalism no-no.

Rule 23 of Professor Clark's rule of journalism states, "You must always ask an open-ended question. One that can elicit several sentences of a response. Never one that can be answered in 'yes' or 'no' statements."

I dodge a pile of apple carcasses swarming with wasps and reach high up for a Fuji apple. A couple nearby us clasps hands. The girl in the couple tips her Panama hat at me. I return her smile, but mine doesn't reach my eyes like hers does.

Let's go for a subject change.

"So, Tony, what's your favorite apple and why?"

Good, a why question.

He sniffs and rubs the bottom of his nose with his index finger. "Don't have a favorite."

My skin sizzles. And because this gingham dress takes on breezes and airiness well, we can't darn well blame the sun for that. "Oh, what's your least favorite one?"

"Dunno."

Oh my word, Johnny, why did you set me up on a date with this bozo? Sure, he has cute blue glittering eyes and a sharp jawline. Sure, those biceps could give an arm wrestler a heart attack.

But come to think of it, Johnny's eyes don't go too many shades beyond his. And I know that Johnny hits the gym for arm workouts at least two or three times a week.

Johnny, you might as well have put me on this date with you. Based on this criteria.

I shake away the thought and fail to reach a Fuji apple on the topmost branch. Wispy clouds dot the cerulean sky.

Him and I—Johnny, I mean—had considered dating for a while. Plenty of ladies in the church asked when we'd finally get together. But with him and I giving dating apps a try for a few years, and with him taking a job out-of-state for another two ... the timing never worked out.

So by now, eight years have passed.

"Let's give Granny Smith a try, eh?" I suggest this for the hopes that Rose and Johnny tarried behind. Then we can "accidentally" bump into them, and I can find refuge in a conversation with one of them.

Tony shakes his head and shoves his hands into his jeans pockets. "Golden Delicious."

I hold in a breath and release it all the way to the end of the row. "Fine. That sounds fine."

We cram our way into Golden Delicious Lane. Plenty of

couples, families, and others laden with baskets have chosen this row. Makes sense. They recognize the name more than other more obscure ones like "Catshead" or "Kanzi."

After we venture far enough down the path, we manage to locate a tree with some fruit left on it. He plucks some small, weak bulbs and drops them into the basket. The weight pulls down my arm. Goodness, I could use some elote right now.

I shut my eyes and try to envision Johnny having a good time on his date. Maybe I need to switch tactics in our conversation.

"So, Tony, I mentioned back in the car that I was once in journalism, but am now working as the Communications Director at our local church. What questions do you have for me?"

Sometimes Johnny doesn't like talking about himself. So he'll throw some questions my way to get our conversation going. Of course, a few paragraphs in, he finds a rhythm in the dance of tête-à-tête.

"I don't think I have any."

My grip tightens on the basket strap. "Okay, then."

For the next twenty minutes, we carry on in silence. Him meandering in rows and choosing apples. Me accepting them without a word.

Relief causes me to gasp when I feel my pocket buzz. A text from Johnny about grabbing some food, winks on the screen.

I seize Tony's arm and make a sprint for the food stalls, dragging him along with me. Some apples trundle out of the basket, but Lord knows, by this point I don't care. We spot Rose and Johnny in a line for apple cider donuts. Johnny's shoulders, hiked up to his ears, drop when he glimpses us.

"Ah, Elise." He grips the apple basket in his hand and gestures at Rose with the other. "Rose was just saying how she wanted a donut. I actually am craving some elote." He gestures at the Mexican street corn food stall. "Tony, mind waiting with Rose?"

Tony shrugs.

In a rapid motion, Johnny snags my arm and pulls me toward the queue for corn. He releases me and a gasp.

"Oh, thank goodness."

I cock my head. "Date not going well?" I set my basket on a picnic bench beside us and promise myself I'll pick it up when the line moves again.

"Elise, you know I love you, but I swear you're trying to murder me."

My nostrils wrinkle, either to sneer or hold back a laugh. Not sure which one. "That's funny, because I was about to say the same thing to you. What went wrong with Rose?"

"What didn't?" He makes a Pac-Man out of his hand. "Talk, talk, talk, talk, talk. It's one thing when I have conversations with you, because you have so many meaningful things to say. But she beat to death the same two topics, and I couldn't get two words in."

I hmm.

"Sorry, my dude, that's unfortunate. I chose her for you because I know you enjoy conversations." But come to think of it, any encounter I *have* had with her, she did like to direct the topic to herself.

"What happened with Tony?"

After my explanation, and us placing our order of corn slathered in mayonnaise and chili powder, we step to the side and wait for our food.

"That's too bad. I'd chosen him for you because I know you like one-on-one time and someone who listens."

"Yeah, dude, when it's with you."

"Yeah, well, I feel the same exact way about you, Elise."

We freeze, eyes wide. A worker shoves two cobs on

sticks at us. We take them and slide onto a picnic bench, batting away bees.

"So." He opens his mouth to bite into the cob, stops, clamps his lips shut. "You're saying that if you could pick someone to be on this date with—"

I snort. "It wouldn't be Tony." I glance at his hand, the trails his veins make, and fight the urge to hold it. "But yes, I'd prefer to be on it with you. To be honest, on most dates I've been on, you've been the standard. And no one measured up. I just—" Deep breath. "—figured we were too late. Eight years, you know? So that's why we picked dates for each other, to find the best replacement we could."

I finger the apples in my basket and try my best to ignore my pounding heart. Fail.

"Maybe."

He chomps into the corn and immediately dabs his lips with a pile of napkins we'd grabbed from the stall. With his free hand, he grabs mine. Relief fills me.

"Or maybe, Elise, we picked just the right timing to choose the right person."

OCTOBER

SCARY LOVE

ROSE HATHAWAY

"YOU'RE GOING TO GET SCARED FIRST, LILITH, AND I'M going to get it on camera."

Hitch lifts his phone flashlight at me in the haunted house, the third one we've tried today. A smirk cuts across my cheek like a slasher's knife.

"Put that thing away. Flashlights are for scaredy cats. And besides, everyone knows you're going to lose the bet."

I pause in a room full of dangling chainsaws, lit by blacklights. Someone wedged in the corner between the fridge and the pantry forgot to put on black shoes today. His white sneakers glow blue in the lighting. "Hey, my dude, may want to try different footwear. Nice job on the makeup though."

A man in a costume, whose face helped itself to tons of lubricant mixed with scarlet dye, heavy-sighs. His shoulders hang as he heaves a chain over it and pads out of the room.

Hitch has turned off his phone. But I catch his pale nostrils wrinkling in the dim room lighting. A mop of black hair, floofed in Edward Scissorhands style, hangs off his head.

"You could've been nicer, Lilith."

"What? You and I have a bet that we'll see as many haunted attractions as possible together, and whoever gets scared first loses. A bet, which, I remind you, has a wager of $200. The most I can ask is that the people hidden in the rooms do a better job in their disguises. You too, Miss My-Hoodie-Strings-Are-White."

A girl in a hoodie scoured with slashes—likely from scissors she used to tear through the fabric earlier—and bloodstains exhales and darts out of the room in the same direction as chainsaw man. Music from the *Halloween* movie soundtrack blasts from some speakers nearby, covering her footsteps.

Hitch shrugs. "I guess that's what you get when you go to a haunted house in someone's neighborhood. Should we ditch?"

I nod. "Yeah. I don't think we're going to have any luck getting goosebumps in here."

He offers his arm, and I feel a rush of adrenaline pump in my neck. But I can't let him see my ... is it fear? Excitement?

Hitch and I have shared a friendship for several years now. Broaching our late twenties, sometime back in high school we met at a Halloween dance in our school gym. Since then, we've caught every so-called "scary" flick in the theater together.

In college, we dressed up as popular horror characters at Cedar Point for a fall job.

And when Hitch entered grad school, we managed to book plenty of gigs as blood-splattered workers in a haunted maze.

Nothing scares us ... Well, nothing except any time we initiate any sort of physical contact.

Electricity brushes my fingertips as I loop my arm into his.

"Where to next?" I try to keep my voice high and cheery so he doesn't catch the quiver at the back of my throat. I figure I can blame it on the chilly night that skirts our ankles.

Never mind that I've donned a full long-sleeved Morticia Adams dress that moves on the driveway like liquid. Nah, that excuse won't work, will it?

"Well it's starting to get dark, so we could try one of the outdoor haunted sites."

"Haunted maze?" I ask, slipping my hand out of his arm, hoping he doesn't notice.

My arm hates the feeling when we break touch.

Hitch and me. Me and Hitch. Not that we didn't give whatever we were a try. In the middle of the most recent horror movie a few months ago, he did lean in for a kiss. But I froze. And buried my face into our tub of popcorn.

He and I pretended the whole thing didn't happen.

A scream pierces my thoughts as kids in trick-or-treat outfits skitter past, pillow cases sailing in the wind. We climb into his car, parked at the base of the driveway from the neighborhood haunted house. Purple and blue lights blare on the siding of the house. Some kind of ghost projection moves back and forth on the roof, the shingles covered in cobwebs.

"Haunted maze it is." He clicks the keys into the ignition. "But of course, some tunes to get you in the I'm-going-to-pee-my-pants mood."

He scrolls on a Spotify playlist and taps the soundtrack from *Coraline*.

"You wish." I chuckle and stare at the window. Hitch

has his arm to the side, laying slack against the side console.

Memories blur back to the day right before the incident at the movie theater.

We'd gone to a Harry Potter event together, dressed as Sybill Trelawney and Snape. Our local downtown ran the whole shebang. Coffee shops boasted of the newest Butterbeer recipes, and every sidestall known to man crowded Main Street with supposed haunted journals, vials full of protective charms, and knitted black cats.

I poked my straw through a domed cup full of blended Frappuccino-style butterbeer as Hitch managed to snag a spot underneath a weeping willow planted near the abandoned railroad tracks.

He patted the ground beside him and flicked the greasy dark wig hair out of his face.

I liked looking at his face. So I forced myself to stare at the whirls of whipped cream instead.

"Lilith, can you believe that we've known each other for ten whole years?" He leaned his head back against the tree, his wig getting stuck on one of the nooks in the trunk.

"Yeah. Crazy."

I crossed my legs in my patchwork skirt, curly, frizzy Trelawney wig obscuring my face.

Ten years of him comforting me through some painful breakups. The most recent one being a man who stalked me to kingdom come. I had to block him on all social media channels, change my name online, and even move to a new apartment. Couldn't be too cautious with a type of man like that.

Give me any horror movie villain, any Freddy Krueger, any Pennywise, I could handle that.

But touching any man after a boyfriend like that could give a girl shivers.

"We're here." Hitch's voice in the car yanks me back into the present.

Craving the aftertaste of butterbeer from the memory, we stop by a stall at the entrance of the maze offering hot drinks. After downing some cinnamon cider and chewing our way through some fresh roasted corn cobs, we plunge into the maze.

The whole time, I watch as Hitch's hand dangles off to his side, ready for me to snatch.

Strobing lights dot my vision as a man with an ax raised above his head yells at us from one of the corners of the maze.

"Great hiding spot," I inform him.

His shoulders slump, disappointment etching onto his face covered in fake scars. He tries one more wimpy "aaaah" and then shrinks back into his corner.

"Maze not doing it for you either?" Hitch asks. We dodge to the side as a woman in a costume from *The Ring* crawls past us. How did she see with so much hair covering her face?

"We only got one last thing on the list, right?"

"Uh huh. Madison Seminary. Most haunted building in this fine state."

Ah yes, Ohio did boast of a two-hundred-year-old building full of ghosts and who-knows-what horror unleashed from the building's past. According to some videos I scrolled past on social media, the building once served as a psych ward for female patients. Images of lobotomy chairs and claw marks on doors skittered past my vision at the memory.

"Ready to get scared out of your wits, Hitch?"

"Funny, I was going to ask you the same thing."

We drive to the building—by now it's early evening—shrouded in darkness. I get so giddy this time of year about how much the wind howls and the pale moon glints in the sky like a corpse.

Lights glint against the pillars of the old brick building. Hitch pats my shoulder, and I flinch.

"Ready?"

I love and hate myself for how much my skin warms at his touch. "Haha. Of course. Let's start with the fourth floor first."

He frowns, door ajar. "The fourth floor?"

"It's where the psych ward was. If we're gonna get scared, it's gonna happen up there."

He grins. "I'm game."

We slam the doors shut and enter the chilly building. I've heard that bricks hold the cold, but I didn't expect the circulation in my fingertips to get cut off. Maybe some ghosties have decided to play with some of our organ functions.

Not that Hitch and I haven't run into some ghoulies in our yearly searches for haunted attractions. I remember one with a blue face at the base of my bed in a haunted hotel I stayed at once.

We wind up echoing staircases, breaths getting caught by the sheer number of steps. Dragon puffs of smoke blow through my lips as I can feel them already chapping. Dang, I can see my breath inside this building.

I shove my hands underneath my armpits as we reach the fourth floor. We traverse the halls full of peeling wallpaper and approach a large room with a window. Shattered glass litters the floor nearest a lobotomy chair.

"Women used to wave to their neighbors out that window." I gesture at the now-dark pane, imagining what it would be like in the daylight of the twentieth century.

When mothers would threaten to send their children to the "nuthouse" if they didn't behave.

His shoulder brushes mine as he stares at the window. "I imagine they must've been really scared."

His touch. I forget how to breathe.

"Y-yeah."

"You okay?"

"Y-yeah, just cold. It's really cold in here. I've lost circulation in my hands."

"Here. Mine are warmer. I can warm them up for you."

I flinch and pull my hands back as he moves to rub them in his.

"I—I'm sorry. You won. I'm scared."

Moonlight from the window highlights his frown. "I'm confused. We haven't even gotten to the scary part of the building. Did you *see* those haunted dolls in the room on the ground floor?"

When we entered the building, the workers had us sign a waiver that stated something along the lines of, "Yeah, our ghosts are kind of malevolent, blah, blah, blah. They may hurt you, blah, blah, blah. We're not responsible for that, blah, blah, blah."

As I signed, a menagerie of ancient dolls with milky white eyes stared me down.

A shiver overtakes me on the fourth floor. "I—just am scared, okay?"

"Okay." He draws back. Then his features soften. "Lilith, are you—are you scared of me?"

"I." I sigh. Slump to the floor, floorboards creaking beneath me. "I don't want to be. You've been so patient with me, not making a move after the whole movie theater thing, but." Tears prick the corners of my eyes. "I want—you." I finish the sentence on a lame note.

He waits.

"But, Hitch, I'm scared what will happen if I do. After the last guy—"

Words catch in my throat, choking me.

He squats, reaches forward with a hand, then pulls it back. "Lilith, to be honest, I'm scared too."

I glance at him through a blur of moisture.

"Y-you are?"

"Yeah. We've been friends for so long. Of course I'm scared. What if I mess it up? What if I ruin both a friendship and something more? That sort of stuff is scary."

My knuckles move to the corners of my eyes. "So I guess we both lost the bet?"

He plops onto the floor and wraps his arms around his knees. "Yeah, I guess we did."

We sit in silence for a few moments as the muffled screams from downstairs fill the space between us. Warmth overtakes me, and I reach for his hand.

"Hitch?"

"Hmm?"

"I don't think I'm so scared anymore."

NOVEMBER

♥ ♥ ♥

THE VETERAN'S DAY DANCE

RENEE LEONARD KENNEDY

THE SMOKY MOUNTAINS SHUDDERED WITH LEAVES TWO weeks before the arrival of fall. The waters flowing past the Deep Creek General Store were cold now, and Liv had deflated all but ten inner tubes. Some of the college crowd braved the ride from the upper Smokies back to the store, but most preferred to stay dry.

She glanced across the way to her competitor, Creekside Lodge. The owner, Axel Reed, lived up to his name, slicing a log into halves with one swing. He lowered the axe and picked up an indulgence of firewood—the show-off. Liv enjoyed her ninety-second romances with him. No fights, no infidelity, no loneliness. Pure-hearted joy shot through her veins. Hope and endorphins and the surprise run-ins with Axel had carried her throughout her two years as manager of the lodge.

"Coming to the campfire tonight?" Axel asked this.

Tossing an oak branch into her campground's fire pit, Liv wondered if one day she'd wade the creek over to his side and go more than a ninety-second round. But until the store and grounds showed profit, she'd remain solo. "Game night again." Mr. Winesap would be undone if he didn't get a dose of Yahtzee.

"If you can sneak away, the invitation remains." Axel stacked the wood in his cut off sweatshirt. The Semper Fi tattoo followed the line of his tricep. Safely separated by the creek, she admired his power and his know-how, among other attributes. Two ninety-second romances in one day. Not a record, but invigorating all the same.

If Axel wasn't so neighborly, she could be mad about the upgrades and activities he offered. Instead, she waved him goodnight. Liv glanced behind him. Sure enough, the Vanmeters's—her customers—were parked in his campground next to the lodge. Romancing was fine, but stealing long-time customers wasn't. "Good rotten night," she whispered.

Axel whipped on his flannel. No doubt the sweat sharpened the lines of his muscularity.

Coffee and estrogen would right her thinking. Layered warm, Liv hopped on her bike and headed the two miles to Bryson City, bypassed by the cars coming off the mountain.

The title papers came today. Liv was now the official owner of the Smoky Mountain campground and its store. But what should've signaled celebration only reminded her of loss.

Aunt JoAnne had been gone a year now. Living without Jo in the world, let alone in the place her aunt had loved the most, made Liv understand why leaves gave up green for gold, then rusted. Her world was falling. Scattered as the wind, Liv pumped her legs faster. She needed to plan, something she used to do. But no longer. Now, life was one emergency agenda after another. Necessary upgrades and people choosing to vacay at home had cash running thin with winter on the horizon. Liv needed another source of income.

The shop bell rang. The rhythm of the coffee shop comforted her. Good, Janice was here. Her friend looked up from the espresso machine. "Same old, Liv?"

Liv swished her mouth. "An extra shot of espresso, I think."

"Wires you too much, friend."

"Says the woman who has a fiancé." Liv fell onto the couch. She thought by thirty she'd be more financially secure. She'd been in her mid-twenties, editing technical literature for a firm in Charlotte. Then the cancer had drained her aunt of time, energy, and money, and Liv had come to help. She felt a similar drainage now.

"Looking glum." Barb, the owner of the coffee shop, settled beside her.

"I'm grateful," Liv said.

"There's a but in your voice."

"Love the store and the grounds during the season—so much to do. The many people I meet. The fun customers have tubing down the mountain. Or spending their vacation fishing. But the new gravel, bathroom upgrades, the stinking Wi-Fi."

"Cleaned your accounts?" Barb asked.

Liv didn't have the energy to agree.

"You should have seen that place thirty years ago. It was hopping. Famous people rode the tubes down."

Janice handed Liv her coffee and joined them on the couch. "Billy Graham preached there in the early days, my grandpa said."

"Walt Disney visited before Disneyland," Barb added. "Jo had so many pictures of the early days."

Liv sipped her drink. "How do I make the campground a place to go again?"

"Nature's done quite a fine job of it." Barb patted her knee.

"But Axel's bringing them in. An actual mini-bus load."

"You don't have a lodge, Liv," Janice said.

"But there has to be something to scrounge up some extra funds."

"Let's make a list," Barb said.

"I'll grab the paper." Janice jumped up, unbalancing Liv on the lumpy couch.

"Barb, I can't afford to upgrade the Wi-Fi until next year. I need an idea. Axel does campfires. Just campfires, and yet people flock to him. Surely I can do better."

"Axel tells stories. He's a former marine. The veterans love him."

Janice handed Barb a legal pad and a Sharpie.

"Don't try to beat Axel." Barb numbered a blank list one to ten. "Tell me some things only you can do."

Liv recalled her last two years. "I can talk to lawyers and accountants, sign papers. Settle an estate." Bury the most important person in my life, Liv thought. "Tile bathroom floors. Clean a camper. Edit. Proofread."

Barb scratched her nose. "Good." She wrote. "Anything communal in nature?"

Liv wanted to slip between the couch's cushions and join the spare change. "I can teach others to play *Apples to Apples.*"

Holding the marker over the pad, Barb's hand went in a circle. "Come on with me." They hunkered low to go to the second story. The door creaked open. Pitch blackness hid the two.

"Swat for the string to the lightbulb," Barb said.

While fearful of the spiderwebs, Liv hated the dark more. She arched her arms, pulling away at the first touch of a cord, then snagged the string. Light filled the space, showing boxes of all sizes and kinds.

Liv sneezed. "You could Airbnb this. After a clean-up."

"With a six-foot ceiling?"

"Part of the charm?"

"We're looking for a box with a pink lid." Barb toed a shoe box away from their path. "Only on top. Not the sides." Barb started on the right side.

Liv stepped over a rusty bed frame to get to the left side of the attic. "What's in all these?" They would be lucky to find the box in this conglomeration.

"This and that." Barb moved one tower into another, all for the sake of a pink lid. "Jo would be proud of you. You're not backing down. You could have sold."

Liv didn't mention that she'd had the campground appraised for that reason. Nor did she want to admit to Aunt Jo's best friend that nobody seemed a right fit for the sale. Investors came in, but if she sold the grounds, she wanted the property to go to a family, somebody who planned to keep the legacy going. Not turn it into a theme park.

"What exactly is in the box?" Liv started work on her third tower.

"You'll see."

Ready to make an excuse to leave, Liv pushed through to the fifth tower of boxes. There it was. The pink-lidded box was decorated with Auntie Jo's curled script. Ages seemed to have passed since Liv had lived in Charlotte, receiving her aunt's precious letters. "Davy and Jo's Adventures" was marked on the paper, weathered brown with age. "I found it. Uncle Davy. It's been so long since I've spoken his name."

Barb lifted the lid. A sepia-toned photo showed the couple dancing decades before Liv was born.

"The studio. I thanked Auntie Jo for it in our last days together." Moving from city to city with her unsettled and broken mother had weighed on Liv. The common denominator before her life with Auntie Jo had been filthy blankets, empty bottles, and mice droppings.

"What a day it was when Jo picked you up for good." Barb picked another photograph. "She had worried every day of your life."

At sixteen years old, for the first time in her life, Liv had slept in her own bed, eaten homemade food, and worn new clothing. Auntie Jo had topped the day off by taking her to the most fabulous place in the world, The Kaylor Dance Studio.

"Jo said you hated going there. Hated dancing," Barb said.

"I was a rather ornery teen, wasn't I?" Catching up on school at the studio was embarrassing. Book smart, Auntie Jo had helped. Uncle Davy was fix-it smart, which blessed her grounds now.

"You lit up, your aunt said, when you danced."

"Tried hard not to."

"Dancing has a way to make you forget everything," Barb added.

"Giving up the studio's lease was hard." There was no way to run the studio from Charlotte. Liv didn't have time. Her Auntie Jo hoped Liv would become a dance teacher. Uncle Davy wanted her to run the campground. One of them got his way in the end.

Barb shook a photograph at her. "This might be your answer."

In the picture, Liv, decked out in an elaborate costume, danced with Mr. Ingalls. She had picked up the sport quickly. Being at the studio every weekday until ten helped. "I haven't danced in a decade."

"What about a dance hall? Lessons?" Barb pecked at the picture with her index finger.

"Adding a studio rental is the opposite of what I want to do."

Barb dug deeper into the box and unearthed a pair of dance shoes. "Jo brought this box from the studio the day they moved out. I was told then to give you these. Your aunt should have put it in her will instead of my memory." She handed the shoes over to Liv.

Her finger followed the shoe's arch. She tugged at the snap. "I loved the waltz."

"The rumba too, if I recall," Barb added.

Liv shuffled through the box. A laminated news-clipping of her uncle's obituary appeared. "'Uncle Davy who was in the Navy,' Auntie Jo used to say."

The day of his burial was fresh still, even though she was eighteen then. The color guard's march down the church aisle. The trumpet's cry of "Taps." The flag's precise folding. Liv had first experienced the smallness of Auntie Jo, bent over the flag given to her, speaking her husband's name.

Liv checked her watch. "I need to get back for check-in, or they'll abandon me for Axel's place." Although the leaves looked far more gorgeous where her grounds—their grounds—were. She had to fight for her guests. "It would require a lot of work, but maybe."

"A mile ahead of me, Liv. What is 'it'?"

"A month until Veterans's Day. Remember the big room Auntie Jo used for storage? It's big enough. I could clean it out, string some lights, borrow heaters. Voilà. A dance floor."

"Ten dollars a head," Barb stated.

"People will pay?"

"To get out of the house in November? You betcha."

"My dance card isn't overwhelmed with people, Barb."

"Bill it as a community event. Even Mayor Heath would show."

"How many people you think?" Liv asked.

Barb tongued her cheek. "Maybe seventy-five. Then you can get a portion signed up for privates."

Staying behind someone's page by proofing and editing was safe. Liv was more comfortable when her auntie had stepped into the limelight. The last time she'd danced, her mother had shown up drunk. Hard to forget as a seventeen-year-old.

She helped Barb off the floor, pecked her on the cheek, and tucked the box of pictures and shoes against her side. "Once a month, and I can pay for the Wi-Fi."

"Once a month, and we'll get this whole town dancing." Barb shimmied her shoulders.

Strapping the box to her bike, Liv welcomed the idea of getting her brakes fixed on the truck. Could this idea be profitable? "Wish me well. I'm going into the enemy's camp."

Liv Bright Johnson had never been to Axel's lodge or campgrounds office. At the moment, he was hefting a cooler through the campground. The man moved so much he never required a jacket. The beginnings of the campfire caught the blonde-red glints in his hair. If she didn't have an agenda, Liv would stand there and add more seconds to her romance count.

"Hello, Liv." He moved a log with his bare hands. Her throat made a noise. Axel squared up to her.

"Did you sigh?" Axel raised his chin.

"A breathing exercise. I forgot to practice it this morning." Liv was reminded of another reason she loved the ballroom. Dancing was filled with the promise of completing old steps, learning new ones, and the anticipation of whether she'd be able to pull all the pieces together. Dancing with the opposite sex, older or younger, never felt awkward because it was about the movement. Talking to this man was different. She reverted to her teenage self, hiding from Axel like she had an acne breakout.

A dance hall would put Mr. Axel Reed right where he belonged: an ebullient student and leader to dance with other women.

"I'd like to honor the veterans."

He rolled his sleeves up. "That's interesting."

"I'm sure you're wondering how."

"I'm sure I'd like to hear," he said.

Liv calculated the time needed to unclutter the storage area, plus clean campers and manage the store. She'd have to get extra hands. "Will you help me out?" After the clean-up, three weeks would remain to teach Barb, Janice, Mayor Heath, and she hoped Axel, the basic steps of the waltz and the rumba.

"Will you quit staring at the campfire from across the creek and join me?" Axel asked.

"I don't stare."

"I beg to differ." Axel crossed his arms.

Auntie Jo said you give a little to get a little. "After I get the games going, I'll come back."

"I'll be waiting."

Turned out, Mr. Winesap's gout bothered him, and Liv led the games. She handed Yahtzee over to Mrs. Cox, who had been longing to take over game night. As she scooted over the bridge, Liv noted the dying campfire and a lone man in an Adirondack chair. Liv stopped. His head leaned back, as if sleeping. She was tempted to turn around.

He had to be cold only in a flannel shirt. She leaned down to see if he had fallen back to sleep. The world spun like a Viennese waltz. In an over-calculation of distance, her shoes met his. They'd never been this close. She unraveled a blanket and eased the fabric over his body.

"Been waiting." Axel's eyes were still closed. "The blanket was for you."

Liv stopped gawking. Other than Auntie Jo, no one had ever thought of her being warm or cold. She took a step back.

The shiver racing through her would not be warmed by a blanket. Axel Reed was not someone to be treated lightly. "I'll go so you can sleep." She spun around, but he grasped her hand.

"My eyes are opened. Will you sit with me?"

From the few years of dance she'd had, Liv was used to touching in a technical manner. His hand holding hers jarred her awake. The touch of another, but a man like no other, was something to behold.

Axel nodded toward their hands. "Quite a grasp you have there."

Unclenching her grip, Liv's fingertips skimmed his worked skin. "I've lost my gentle touch, it seems." She landed hard onto a bench, rocking it backwards. He stomped his foot on the seat to prevent her from overturning.

She straightened her posture. "I'd like to honor the veterans with a dance."

"Hello to you too." He rested his chin on his fist.

"We can talk tomorrow."

"Tonight's fine. Good idea. Most of my people, and the community, would rally," he said.

"How about you?"

"I'll have to see."

Liv kicked at his hikers. "I didn't know how to dance either." She had never flirted with a man, and yet here she was. "Auntie Jo taught me. You can learn."

"I heard the story of you two at her funeral."

"You were there?"

"You might not have noticed, but the whole town was. I hadn't seen you since you were eighteen." Axel Reed tapped her hikers back. "Then you were busy with the campground."

Working the grounds had numbed her. Liv had focused on memories of Auntie Jo because she didn't want to forget. This was the lightning strike needed to make her look at the beauty, not just the work, surrounding her.

The fire popped, and a cinder landed on Axel's jeans. He flicked the unwelcomed visitor away. "How can I help?"

Axel Reed had only grown more attractive in the last couple of months. It was a mystery how she could see him off and on, from being a young soldier to a seasoned retired one, and not noticed whenever she made pit stops at the grounds. Brokenness had damaged her. Living in the wreckage of her mother's all-consuming addictions had only taught Liv to hold on loosely. To avoid direct personal communication, most especially with men. Could she dance with him?

No denying Liv could stay with Axel for the rest of her life in more than a ninety-second romance. But would he dance with her? Perhaps if they worked side-by-side, he'd be more willing to give the waltz a chance. "Help me clean out the storage?" Her voice lowered at the uncertainty of her plan.

"You finally make it over to my campfire for that?" He glanced through the dark night to the stars.

"And set it up for a Veteran's Day dance?"

His body seemed to deflate. Axel dropped his palms to his knees. "Need decorations, I suppose."

They stared at each other. Liv wanted to name exactly what she wanted. A deep-felt tango. But she either should run toward him or away, and she had no idea which.

"Tomorrow good?" Axel shuffled the coals with a stick to coax the fire.

The embers awoke. Liv lowered her tense shoulders. "That would be great."

The next day, the rotted floor was not so great. Axel and she discovered a leaky roof had weakened boxes of old dishes, sheets, and towels. Even canned coffee.

"I knew it. The roof." Liv shook her head.

"The heavier boxes, I'll get." Axel eyed the ceiling.

"Hope there's no more surprises."

"We'll fix it."

After Liv made them quick sandwiches from last night's meatballs, Axel started repairing the roof with a box of shingles he found. The wood floor crumbled under the pressure of Liv's crowbar. New floor boards were cut, the sweet wood smell covering the must. Hammering created its own rhythm, making Liv excited about dancing again.

"Ten more minutes of your time?" She leaned on the wood frame of the velveteen couch. "Axel, please?"

He paused in packing his gear. "I wanted to help you out. You know that, right?"

Liv gestured to a vintage rug, and then toed the weave open across the floor. "I don't want to be a burden."

"Is that why you never come over?" He picked up the bulk of the couch, leaving Liv to direct with the end she held.

She didn't respond. Auntie Jo and Uncle Davy had welcomed her into their home, odd as living on a campground could be. But by doing so, they'd invited in her mother's chaos, occasional wired visits, and constant requests for money.

He smoothed his hand over the couch's wood arch to grab hers. "It's a pleasure helping you."

They moved a library table in front of the bookcases she'd arranged with books and dance awards her aunt had won, as well as a tea set, all feminine with its light pink roses and delicate china.

"But you don't believe that." Axel filled the door frame, brushing wood chips into the refreshed Mountain Laurel beds. "You don't remember the five times I've invited you over."

"You have not. Once, just yesterday."

"You were sixteen, and I was off for my first tour fifteen years ago. You wouldn't talk to me."

"I talked to nobody."

"Then your first college break and one leave twelve years ago."

"I don't remember that."

"Then I learned you'd brought a guy home."

"Did I?" Liv skimmed through her college years. "Fredrick. We were study partners."

"You two were intense. Just studying?"

"You watched us?"

"Remember how your aunt and uncle were friends with Uncle Oscar? He gave me the lowdown."

"Your uncle, yes." Liv hadn't thought of him in years. He'd hosted Sunday churches on the grounds. Some days he preached to three, on other days fifty. "I never said I'm sorry over his passing."

Axel nodded toward the chairs and table.

"Yes, please," Liv said. "Let's be the first."

Axel pulled out the best chair for her. Her spine leaned into the wood slats. "Then your graduation party."

"You weren't at the studio then."

"I was at the door when Jo spoke." Axel tugged the other chair near her.

"We'd fought. I wanted to visit, not do a showcase. I hadn't practiced in two years."

"Jo wanted the best for you," he said.

Liv smoothed her hand over the water-stained wood. "Such a fuss over my 'surprise' dance partner. It was too much."

The door slammed open. Janice held a slip of paper. "Axel. You're here."

"Look what all he did." Liv waved her arm across the room.

"We did." He nodded to Liv.

"The lighting stinks," Janice added.

"We've got it covered." Axel leaned back, pulling a tall, leather book off the shelves.

"What's the paper?" Liv brushed straying hair from her face, then shook the sweaty shirt from her stomach.

"I came to say hello."

"You never come during coffee hours."

"Trying new things." Janice turned to leave.

Liv hopped up from the chair and snatched the paper from her hand. "What is this?"

Janice snatched it back. "None of your business. That's not true. It is your business. Just not right now."

Axel flipped through a historic map collection. "Best come out with it, Janice."

Liv held her hand out.

Grimacing, Janice placed the paper in her palm. "It was done with good intention."

"1190. Axel Reed."

"What is that?" Axel closed the book.

Janice's shoulders hunched. "The number of coffee beans in the canister."

"But why my name?" Axel asked.

"You correctly guessed the number of coffee beans in the canister."

"Congratulations." Liv passed the note to Axel. "What did he win?"

He smoothed out the paper with his thumb. "I didn't enter this."

"He won dance lessons with you, Liv." Janice grimaced.

She took a step back. "I didn't ask for your help, Janice."

"No, but Barb thought it appropriate." She glanced at Axel.

"Janice, Barb and you need to cease and desist." He grabbed his bag and walked Janice through the door.

Hurrying outdoors, Liv spotted Janice backing up her car and Axel lumbering over the bridge to his place. "Come back!"

He leaned his hands on the wood bridge posts.

Her face reddened from far more than the cold. But she had no other way to find out. "About those lessons."

Axel tilted his face to the sky and mumbled something, the words stolen by the waters rushing beneath him. He jumped over the few steps leading down from the bridge and landed hard on his feet. His equipment bag jangled against his side. He didn't look back.

Every night after her dance lessons with the mayor, Barb, and Janice, she'd venture out to check out the campfire across the way, hoping to see Axel. But the fire pit was banked. If only Barb and Janice hadn't meddled, Liv would have been able to ask him to dance.

Having lost enough sleep, Liv stapled and taped flyers around town. The insurance company bought flags to line the gravel drive in sponsored advertising. Barb provided the coffee, and judges were chosen for the cake competition. Uncle Davy had said Jo's coconut pound cake, which he had called a 'fattycake,' had settled their engagement.

Across the creek, men from the Korean War and onward through history showed Liv pictures of their far younger selves in uniforms. "May I borrow these?" she asked each one. "I'd like to highlight them at the dance." As she set the last of the flag decorations on the small tables donated by the brewing house, she opened the box to her final project. Maybe this remembrance was too much for Axel. Liv had only heard snippets from Auntie Jo of the friends he'd lost, of his narrow escapes.

She clipped photos from seventy decades old, one even older, to the red, white, and blue yarn she'd braided and strung around the walls. She found a photo of her Uncle Davy, all ears and buzzed head, as he shinnied the mast of a ship. She thumbed through more pictures, then slowed.

In black tails, a ten-years-younger Axel dipped Auntie Jo while she wore a tango dress. Another had him dressed in jeans and a flannel, doing the swing. Others showed him dressed to waltz. While Liv had run from that life, Axel had spent his off-duty time dancing with Auntie Jo. She picked up one last picture. Auntie Jo wasn't dancing, but Axel wrapped her up in a hug. That had to be the year Uncle Davy died.

The community had always come together for her aunt and uncle, Axel at the forefront. She flew out of the dance hall, sprinted across the bridge, and stormed his lodge. Behind the check-in desk, Lucinda held down the ledger pages fluttering with the opened door's breeze.

"Where is Axel Reed?"

Lucinda propped her chin on her hand. "You finally want to see him."

"What's with you all?" Liv thumped the desk. "This town. Its innuendos, secrets, mysteries. I wish you all would just speak. Plain. English."

"Where's the fun in that?"

Liv shook her head. "Tell him please. The dance is in three days. And Liv is inviting him. No, say begging his presence."

"So that's how romance goes these days?" Lucinda gave her a tight smile.

Groaning, Liv slammed the door.

Later, in her twirl-ready dress, she slipped on her dance shoes, the ones Auntie Jo had given her at seventeen. After securing the snap, Liv stood up. Would Axel come? He'd do wonders for the event, a dancer and a veteran.

"Who am I kidding?" Liv knew her desire for his presence was more. She wanted to be with him. Her shoe loosened suddenly. She knelt, noticing the snap had broken away from the strap. Instead of this dance coming together as they had with her aunt, this one seemed to unravel and break apart like her shoe.

Her church pumps would have to do. She added Auntie Jo's necklace for good measure, then scooped up the broken shoes.

As she arranged the shoes among the other Veterans Day memorabilia Uncle Davy and Auntie Jo had accumulated, she startled when Axel spoke her name.

She twirled around. "I didn't expect you so soon." Axel wore his steel-toed boots and flannel. The man in the tuxedo was light years away.

"Thanks." He tapped his hand against his leg. "I'm otherwise engaged."

She sucked in her breath. If those words didn't close the door, then she didn't know what would. Her heart raced as it had when she sold off Auntie Jo's car to pay for the new gravel. "Wanted to be neighborly." Liv pretended to arrange the pictures on the wall.

"I remember when Jo bought you these."

Liv faced him. Axel was holding her dance shoe. "My shoes?"

"Your aunt and uncle didn't have a lot of money. But they couldn't wait to get these from the shop in Georgia."

Liv straightened a picture of her aunt and uncle. She wanted to scream her loneliness to the sky, like a packless coyote in winter.

"Got new ones by now, I'm sure," Axel said.

"No, those are it."

"Howdy, Miss Liv. Ready to rumba." The mayor

lumbered into the center of the floor. "Night, Axel." The mayor winked.

"The waltz." She punched the music in, and she positioned her hands on the mayor's left shoulder and right arm. The door squealed. Axel was gone.

The next night, Liv visited the campfire across the creek. But Axel was not there. Mr. George invited her to stay, but she headed back to the empty dance hall. She pressed American flags into tiny oak tree arrangements. She centered the punch bowl. Like the pathetic girl in a prom movie, she waited by the door, overwhelmed by the warm bistro lights and candles, knowing in three hours the room would be filled with couples enjoying themselves, waltz or not.

In keeping with her aunt's tradition, Liv secreted the name of the veteran she'd picked to dance the first dance. She had settled on the mayor. He'd earned the right to lead. She just couldn't get the image of Axel in his tails out of her mind.

The door squeaked. "I meant to oil that."

"I can do this." Axel said.

Axel. His voice reverberated. Liv wanted to shut her eyes because whether he was going to stay tonight or not, she needed to know he'd be across the way. Or she wasn't going to make it through. "Thank you for your service, Axel."

"I have something for you." He touched her knees with his.

Finally, her eyes met his. Then they traveled down his tuxedo to the box in his hands.

"I couldn't get them mailed on time," he said. "So I drove to Georgia."

"That's why you were gone."

"Wouldn't be right without dance shoes. And you noticed I was gone?"

"I've been counting the time you weren't here since I was sixteen." Liv's head went foggy with the honesty. She shouldn't have, but she did. Should have stood, but couldn't.

He knelt beside her. "I've needed to hear those words for a long time."

"You've wanted me to notice you?"

He lifted the lid off the box. "Why do you think I came here during tours?" One shoe was exposed beneath the tissue paper. He reached for her foot. "May I?"

Words evaporated. She nodded.

He slipped off her pump and lifted the black beauty of a dance shoe. "I need to make my feelings for you clear."

The shoes cradled her feet, like his words did to her heart. "And more than ninety seconds please."

He slipped the other shoe on. The leather tingled against her skin as he latched the shoe on. Her back arched five inches.

"I'm completely yours." Axel held his hand out. Liv stepped toward him. Their feet graced the floor, his hold firm, her arms lifted lightly. "I was also your surprise dance partner."

"Auntie Jo knew best." As the winter sun lowered, the waltz carried them forward. Liv breathed her first breath, it seemed, her chest lifting higher as her face neared his, timelessly.

FRIENDSGIVING

ROSE HATHAWAY

"Hey, Selah, thanks for coming to Enemies-giving."

Selah balked at the front steps of her friend's house, AKA the commune. Inside the building, stationed in the middle of Colorado Springs, nine residents filled the various rooms. Aged between twenty-two and thirty-two, these single folks found a camaraderie within these maple-scented walls.

Ah, a candle flickered on a table near the front door. That explained the smell.

Selah stepped inside and kicked off her shoes, cradling the pie dish in her hand.

"Kati, I thought you said this was Friendsgiving."

Kati adjusted the fraying hem on her sweater. A cartoon turkey decorated the front of the fabric. Selah set her pie down next to the candle and adjusted her woolly socks that had slipped too far down her ankles.

"Ah, you must not have gotten the memo."

"What memo?" Selah frowned.

"I know I just moved here, but I guess they have a tradition where they call it 'Friendsgiving' but really, everyone in this house invites their least favorite person in the world."

"I'm sorry, what?" Selah dug an index finger into her ear to procure wax.

Did she hear that right?

"Yeah." Kati motioned her down a thin hallway, toward the basement. "We have our enemy make the same dish we do. So we'll have two mashed potatoes. Two Brussels sprout bakes. And Lord help the poor enemy who made sweet potato casserole, but I'm going to crush her with mine."

Two dishes? One for the enemy, and one for the person who invited them?

Although Selah had her own dealings with her family back home when it came to who made the mac and cheese ... the aunties would claim Selah made hers "too dry" ... never before had she heard like a tradition like this.

Of all her experiences in college, Friendsgiving was a holiday meant for single folks who didn't have a family to share a Thanksgiving with.

But Enemies-giving?

Kati's voice trailed as she bounced down the carpeted steps.

"We don't say who made which one, so they're judged blindly. Whichever gets picked over the two wins."

"Who is your enemy?" Selah's pulse spiked.

"Oh, girl, it's not you. It's that fricken soprano in our community choir, Delilah. Who thinks she should belt all the high notes. She definitely should *not*. Remember what I said? Your enemy will have the same dish as you."

But ... Kati invited her.

When she reached the bottom of the steps, Selah scanned the crowd. Arms were laden with dishes before guests deposited their delicacies onto the clothed ping-pong table. At long last, she spotted another pie dish wrapped in foil.

She eyed the man carrying it.

Dark curly hair, lean frame. She ... did not know this guy at all.

"Kati, who's that?" she asked.

Kati didn't answer because she'd engaged in a side-hug with Delilah. The soprano must not have caught onto the true meaning behind her invitation. Because Selah caught spare bits of conversation like "thank you for inviting me to Friendsgiving."

Firelight flickered underneath a large screen TV that played a football game.

Selah drank in the various smells as she advanced toward her supposed enemy.

She clacked her glass pie dish against a striped towel and shoved a hand in front of his face. "Selah. Nice to meet you."

Embers glowed in her eyes, she could feel them. Would he get intimidated by her glare?

Had she seen him before? He didn't look at all familiar.

His brows furrowed, then sprang apart. He set his pie down and clasped her hand in his.

Dang, what a firm grip.

"Jacy. Is it just me, or are things really tense to you too?" He gestured at the various enemy "couples" throughout the room. Two men wouldn't break eye contact as they snapped celery from a veggie tray nearby the basement kitchen counter.

"I guess people brought a lot of competing dishes." Back to the subject at hand. As an ex-reporter, Selah would dig to the bottom of every story. If Jacy wanted to play hard to get, she'd figure out his game eventually. "Speaking of, have we met before?"

He squinted at her.

Although she never majored in theater back in college, she could tell a bad actor from a good one. And this was a good one. His face mimicked genuine confusion.

"Can't say that I remember that. Which is unfortunate, because I think I'd like to remember any girl who chooses to wear leggings like that."

She glanced down at her outfit. Cartoon turkeys, pies, and autumn leaves bedecked her calves and thighs. She did a curtsy and tried to ignore the fire that filled her cheeks. Was it blushing? Embarrassment?

"You sound jealous."

"I am. I couldn't rock a pair of those on these wimpy legs."

A giggle cracked and died in her throat. No wait, sometimes enemies did this. Flattered you and then caught you off-guard. Maybe he'd planned to chuck her pie on the ground when she didn't watch, and his would win by default.

Nice try, cutie, but I'm on to you.

Something hard clasped her shoulder, and Selah jumped. She followed the arm to its source, Kati.

"Hey, girl, we're about to start trying the dishes. So it's really important that you and this guy." She nodded at Jacy. "Get in on the action. Vote on your favorite one, okay?"

Jacy cocked his head. "Did she just say vote?"

Before Selah could respond to either of them, Kati dashed toward the green bean casserole dishes stationed at the far-right corner of the ping-pong table.

"Okay, everyone gather around and get a spoonful of each casserole onto your plate."

French fried onions and soupy green beans dolloped

onto Selah's dish. She monitored the others and noticed how they put one scoop—the host's—on one side of the plate and the other one—the enemy's—on the other end.

Her fork poked both. One left a horrible burnt taste in her mouth. The other? The perfect amount of soy sauce lingered in the back of her throat.

Okay, so the host clearly won.

"Okay, now that everyone has tried it." Kati pointed at the host's plate. "Who votes for this one?"

Selah's hand itched to raise along with the others, but in her periphery, she glimpsed Jacy's arm going up.

I can't vote the same as my enemy.

On principle, she kept her hand down. She voted for the burnt one.

Kati squinted at her. "Okay, for kicks and giggles will Jeremy and Ben please do rock, paper, scissors?"

Ben must've been the host, and Jeremy the enemy. Or the other way around. They pounded their fists against their palms as Kati sailed over to Selah. She tugged her to the side.

"You doing okay, girl?"

"Just great."

"Okay, because did you happen to taste something in that one green bean dish that we didn't? Is your palette okay?" Kati's brow creased.

Yeah, just gotta make my enemy know I can't vote for him.

"Beginner's nerves." Selah shrugged. "I'm sure I'll do better next round."

A holler indicated Jeremy won the round of rock, paper, scissors. Maybe Kati did this for tradition's sake? Since clearly everyone else voted for the one, that wouldn't end it in a tie, right?

In between each dish, Jacy asked get-to-know-you questions. Selah kept her answers short until he breached the topics of journalism. She couldn't help it. All walls dissolved and she spoke for minutes on end—as Kati sawed through two turkeys—about her love for finding the right information and interviewing as many sources as possible.

Still, each round, she voted against Jacy.

On principle.

They finally reached the sweet potato casserole dishes. Kati made a pointed scoop in a glass dish. Ah, hers. She recognized the dish from a graduation gift Selah had given to her.

Kati's gonna kill me if I don't vote for hers.

Since Jacy *apparently* had an immaculate palette and chose the best dishes each round—and because Selah voted against him—she prayed Kati burned her casserole or something. So by default, Kati would win.

Either case, it appeared that each round ended in rock, paper, scissors, for some reason.

When Selah took a bite of Kati's casserole, the brown sugar melted in her mouth. Oh goodness, how could the other dish compare with this one?

It, umm, didn't.

In fact, somehow Delilah didn't mash her sweet potatoes all the way. They ended up in clumps that got stuck in the back of Selah's throat.

Sure enough, when they voted, though, Jacy's hand sprung up for Kati's dish. Selah kept her eyes pressed to the carpet and chose the next one.

"Oh my lanta." Kati tugged Selah toward the kitchen. She told the rest of the group to talk amongst themselves. When Selah and Kati reached the veggie tray, Kati hissed, "Are you purposefully trying to vote against my housemates? We worked hard on those dishes to show up our enemies, and now we're having to settle for rock, paper, scissor fights."

Selah cocked her head. "I'm sorry. I did want to vote for your dish."

"And you didn't because?" She triangled an arm on her hip.

"Well, because my enemy kept voting for—"

"Hold on." She held up a hand. "Enemy?"

Selah explained that she and Jacy made competing pies. "The thing is, it's unfortunate that he's a sweet guy. Because honestly, Kati, I have no idea how we became enemies in the first place."

Kati pinched the bridge of her nose. "Oh, Selah, no. You and he are our blind judges. We made you both make dishes to avoid suspicion from the other party guests."

What? Selah blinked several times.

"Blind judges?"

"Yeah, basically your two votes are the only ones that count. We're just pretending to vote so it looks real. But if you two vote against each other, we have to—"

"Do rock, paper, scissors," Selah finished for her. "To determine the winner."

So Jacy hadn't sworn vengeance on her.

Butterflies fluttered in her stomach.

Did that mean she could become friends ... or maybe something better with him? He did seem to have a lot of interest in what she did. In her experience, most guys wouldn't ask that many questions, unless ...

Kati and Selah returned to the ping-pong table in time to catch everyone eating a slice of the pumpkin pies. Jacy dolloped whipped cream onto a triangle of pumpkin.

"Yo, Selah, you made this one, right?"

Throat dry, she nodded.

"Well, it has my vote." He winked at her. "But I'm not sure how I feel about you showing up my pie."

Her fingers rubbed up and down her turkey leggings. "Does that make us enemies?"

"Depends." He stabbed his fork into the pie once more. "Do enemies get to meet up for food after being asked to judge dishes at Thanksgiving? Let's say, next Saturday?"

Selah grabbed the pie server and plopped a piece onto a paper plate. "It sure does, enemy."

DECEMBER

JULY IN CHRISTMAS

ROSE HATHAWAY

"YOU'VE GOT TO BE KIDDING ME."

Felicity stared out the window of the beachside home in the Outer Banks. Soft snowflakes cascaded onto the blacktop. Soon little bits of snow would mix with the brown, sandy dunes.

She'd chosen one of the homes closer to the beach on purpose this Christmas.

Not only because the houses came far cheaper during this time of year—as opposed to the heavy vacation season in July—but because her cousins from Raleigh claimed North Carolina could get up into the eighties in the winter.

Guess they lied.

Should've seen it coming. Her cousins did like to pull the occasional prank at family gatherings.

With a heavy sigh, she retreated indoors and went to the palm tree she'd set up on the top floor. Lights hung from the thick-bladed branches. Santa hats decorated the bookshelves, next to sea shells and dried-up starfish carcasses.

"The weather might not be perfect, but at least we're near the beach."

Pancakes sizzled on the upstairs grill. She'd spritzed peppermint essence into the batter to get a Christmas-y flavor.

As she flipped one over, the doorbell rang. Brows furrowed, she clicked off the burner. No sense in charring her breakfast over some mysterious visitor. A crackling radio nearby played

"Chestnuts Roasting On An Open Fire."

She sailed down two flights of stairs before she reached the front door. Swinging open the knob, she found a man with platinum blonde hair in a thick, wooly blue jacket. He shivered on the doorstep, carrying a plate of saran-wrapped cookies in hand.

"Can I help you?"

"Name's Jack." He handed her the plate of cookies. "Figured you could use this, being one of the only vacationers."

A thin Southern accent played on his lips. Must've been a resident, unlike Felicity with her thick nasal coming out of her mouth.

"Felicity. Thanks." She moved to shut the door, but he'd already stepped inside.

Southern hospitality expectations, perhaps? Or maybe because he hadn't gotten used to the cold.

Oh well, no time for questions. She had a pancake to flip.

She traversed the two staircases and rushed to the griddle. Thank goodness the remaining heat on the skillet managed to cook the other side of the pancake. She slid the breakfast onto a plate and carried the dish to the table. Flamingos in Santa hats stood next to the salt and pepper shakers.

"Sorry for barging in like this." Jack now leaned against the banister on the top floor. "Just not used to the cold. It's a good half-mile walk from here."

Coming from a place like New York City, alarm bells often rang in Felicity's head about types of guys who would barge into homes with sinister intentions. But something about the warmness of his voice and the easiness of his smile set her stomach at ease.

"Peppermint pancakes?" she asked.

Chocolate sauce drizzled onto her stack.

"Had breakfast already, thank you." A low whistle carried through his teeth. "I hope you don't mind me asking, but what are you doing in North Carolina this time of year?"

"July in Christmas." She sat at the table and sawed a triangle into her pancake.

"Do you mean Christmas in July?"

He shed his coat and placed it on the banister. Then he headed to the turquoise loveseat and plopped into the soft cushions. Felicity swallowed a mouthful of warm, minty goodness before pointing her fork at him.

"Nope. July in Christmas. I make a habit of not celebrating *Christmas* Christmas, but variations of it."

"Really?" He rubbed an index finger under his sharp chin.

Gosh dang it, those blue eyes could swallow her whole.

"Well, why didn't you head some place warmer like Florida?"

"Too crowded this time of year," she said.

New York already burst at the seams in terms of population during non-Christmas months. Let alone the people who came from all over the world to gawk at the large trees in Rockefeller Square.

"Hawaii?"

"Too expensive. My ex ..."

She didn't finish. Why would she force Jack to endure some sad sob story about how her ex, three Christmasses ago, conned her out of all her money? And even with three years waitressing and splitting an apartment with three other ladies, she'd barely made a dent in her debts.

"So you settled on North Carolina, huh?"

Silly of her to even bring a surfboard along with her. Why hadn't she checked the weather?

Oh yeah, because her ex had resurfaced in her texts. Claiming he and his new girlfriend had gotten themselves into financial trouble.

He pulled that the year before, claiming his son from another mother needed help to get through a private school—one of the most prestigious in New York.

And the year prior to that, his mother came down with some "mysterious illness."

Instead of going for a St. Patrick's Christmas this year, she gathered her Christmas decorations, bought a few more on Amazon, and booked a ticket for North Carolina. If she claimed she was out-of-reach via cell service—a lie, because the Outer Banks had full signals—maybe he'd leave her alone this time.

"You mentioned you've done different themes in the past?" Jack's voice broke up her thoughts.

"Yes, I have some videos if you'd like to see." She set down her fork on the rest of the pancake stack and ambled toward him.

He scooted to the edge of the loveseat to allow a few inches of space between them. Butterflies fluttered through her stomach as she parked beside him. Something about his piney scent ebbed all anxiety.

Her ex would never wear a cologne like that. He'd always favored strong, musky tones.

"Okay, so this was the theme from last year."

Felicity tapped on the video.

The cameraman, her niece, traversed the dimly lit hallways. She'd snagged a massive deal on renting out a haunted hotel for her Halloween-in-Christmas celebration. And collected admission at the door.

As a zombie, Felicity lurched at the camera. Jack jumped.

"Man, that bloody makeup sure is realistic."

"Thanks, I did feel bad about making that one man cry, though."

A man bundled himself into the fetal position after he ran into the undead Felicity. It took the man's girlfriend a few minutes to get him to lift himself from his "hiding place" and make their way to the exit.

"Those cobwebs look so realistic." Jack didn't sound disgusted. Rather, intrigued. He'd leaned closer to the phone to take in all the details. Once the video finished, he glanced up at Felicity. "What other themes have you done?"

"Well, I do have pictures from the Thanksgiving Christmas, but I got to say, it was less successful than the Halloween one."

Her thumb scrolled through a camera roll from two years back. Family members held up plates full of turkey and cranberry sauce. Her uncle even wore an "Ugly Thanksgiving Sweater" to mark the occasion.

"How so?"

"My family thought I'd just forgotten to do Thanksgiving and was making up for it in December. They didn't really seem to catch on to the fact that I wasn't celebrating Christmas-proper, but my own version."

Perhaps in an instinctual motion, Jack's arm draped over the back of the couch. "Why *do* you celebrate Christmas like this?"

Felicity fought the urge to lean into him and cuddle.

"It's—" She drew her knees to her chest. "Complicated."

"Looks like it's snowing pretty good out there, so we got time."

Flurries fluttered outside the large windows and wet the wooden decks.

Felicity imagined it didn't precipitate like this often in the south. Of all the years, the Carolinas decided to deliver her a white Christmas.

"My ex, he ... really loved Christmas. We'd go all out. Ugly sweaters, white elephant gift exchanges—we even did that German tradition where you hid a pickle ornament in a tree."

And whoever found the "pickle" would get to open an extra gift. Hidden by Felicity's niece, the pickle was located by her ex first. He refused to take the extra present though. Instead, he kissed Felicity on the forehead and whispered, "You are a gift enough."

Two hours later, when he went to the restroom and left his phone on the couch, she discovered a new text message from a girl named "Tara." When she swiped open the phone ...

Tears itched her eyes. She didn't want to relive those messages. The fact that even though she thought he'd propose to her that Christmas, he'd actually been engaged to another girl that whole time.

She blew out a shaky breath. "Let's just say that celebrating Christmas like other people do reminds me too much of him. So I took the holiday back, made it my own, and celebrate variations of it each year."

Felicity held in a breath.

This part tended to scare away lots of guys. Even though she experimented with the dating scene, they always ghosted after they discovered about her ex. Perhaps perceiving her as too naive, or too broken.

"Well, Felicity, I'm sorry that happened to you. If it's any consolation, my ex was also obsessed with all things Christmas, so I don't even have a wreath up this year." He lifted himself from the couch and stroked the palm tree strung in lights. "This feels more like it."

Tension released from Felicity's shoulders. This one didn't run away.

"Any other July-in-Christmas traditions?" he asked while placing one of the starfish onto the hilt of the tree.

"Let's see. Today's itinerary is creating a sandman—a sandy version of a snowman—making sand angels, and drinking iced mulled wine. Although with how cold it is outside, that wine might be steamed instead."

"Planning to celebrate with anyone?" A twinkle ignited his pupils.

Her lips curved upward in a smirk. "I think I have an idea of who can attend the festivities."

ABOUT THE AUTHORS

(IN ALPHABETICAL ORDER BY LAST NAME)

FELICIA FERGUSON achieved master's degrees in Healthcare Administration and Speech-Language Pathology, but has written since childhood and dreamed of authoring books that teach and inspire others. An award-winning fiction and non-fiction freelance writer, she is the current president of the Destin chapter of Word Weavers International, a writers critique group, and a member of the American Christian Fiction Writers Association. She has previously published devotionals with *Christian Devotions* and *Inkspirations,* and her first contemporary women's novel with End Game Press, *The Choices She Made,* released in 2022.

ROSE HATHAWAY is a pseudonym for Hope Bolinger, who writes way too many books. She's the Managing and

Acquisitions Editor at End Game Press and Generation Hope. Twenty-one of her books are under contract, and she's contributed to twelve others. You can find 1,400 of her bylines in various publications from Crosswalk.com to HOOKED, reaching millions of readers per year. When she isn't dressing up in a pseudonym or costumes in public, you can find her on local runways or getting lost in Ohio's Metroparks. Find more about her at hopebolinger.com

RENEE LEONARD KENNEDY, as many writers do, remembers writing as one of her first memories. After decades of wandering, she came back to words, first in the white space of her Bible, then in stories and ideas. She thanks God for family, friends, acquaintances, once-in-a-lifetime encounters, and books. Writing and reading, working her farm, and being with her adult kids to further their entrepreneurial spirits blesses her heart. Gathering around the table or fire pit with loved ones is her life's pinnacle. Renee is active with Triad Coalition for Life, Save the Storks, Sister Keepers, and Pleasant Garden Baptist Church. She is a new board member to The Oaks Community, a non-profit organization with a focus on mental health and wellness, serving the Piedmont Triad and partners nationwide (www.theoakscommunity.org). The first and last word on her is that she's a follower of Jesus Christ.

LORI Z. SCOTT loves a challenge, which is how she ended up running 5Ks in her 50s (and winning a few), teaching elementary kids for over twenty years (without losing her sanity), doodling cartoons (upside down with both hands at the same time), and cooking dinner (and utterly failing.) In the process of tackling all those challenges, Lori accidentally published a bestselling, ten-title chapter book series and deliberately published over 175 articles, short stories, poems, and devotions. Her latest triumph—besides not catching the oven on fire—is *Inside the Ten-Foot Line,* the first book in a new YA sports series published by End Game Press. Most of Lori's work is marked by humor, including her foray (my, that sounds flirty, doesn't it?) into romance writing. After all, what good is a challenge without a little fun?

Made in the USA
Columbia, SC
24 September 2023

23265643R00124